Star Mote Castle

Ron Mueller

Books and Stories by Ron Mueller
The Taelo Series
Taelo: The Early Years
Taelo: The Golden Feather
Taelo: Journey of Discovery
Taelo: Dangerous Passage
Taelo: Condor Clan Slingers
Taelo: Circumvention
Taelo: The Journey of Sages
Taelo: Collection

A Taelo Story:
White Swan and Quiet Pheasant
The Child's Name
Floating Cloud
Quiet Rabbit
Busy Bee
Little Otter & Talking Wren
Broken Spear
Burley Bear & Meadow Flower

Other books by Ron Mueller
The Door Series:
    The Door
    Delivery
    Journey Beyond
The Savitar Series:
    Journey's End
    Savitar
    Confluence
The Problem Solver Series
    Solutions
    Drug Lords
    Border Crosser

The Alex Evercrest Series:
The River Front
The Girl on The Grill
Missing
Maggot
Racist
Votive Candles
Windy City
Country Road
Pool of Blood
Sins of the Daughter
Body Parts

Single Science Fiction Books:
Current Past and Future
The Event
The Door
Viajante 7

Imagination by Courtney Huynh and Chloe Parker

Star Mote Castle
By: *Ron Mueller*

Around the World Publishing LLC
4914 Cooper Road Suite 144
Cincinnati, Ohio 45242-9998

This story is a work of fiction. Names, characters, places, and incidents either are products of the author's imagination or are used fictitiously. Any resemblance to actual events or locales or persons, living or dead, is entirely coincidental.

Star Mote Castle, Copyright © 2023

ISBN 13:978-1-68223-992-6

ISBN 10: 1-68223-992-6

Distributed by Ingram
Cover Design by: Ron Mueller

Ron Mueller

Table of Content

<u>Chapter 1: The Castle Origin</u>

The warm early summer sun's rays seemed to lazily find their way through the puffy clouds that were slowly floating on the gentle morning breeze. The clear dark blue waters of the river flowed smoothly past on its way toward the sea that was at least seven days away. A small part of the river was diverted to the point where a rotating bucket lift powered by two persons who continuously walked on rotating steps to lift the water up to the mote around Star Castle.

The land north, south, east, and west as far as the eye could see and well beyond was held by Knight Gerrit Van Gesterte. He in essence was the king of this vast area. He had a small force of knights under his command that he used to keep all the serfs in check. He rewarded his knights well. They received a stipend in gold, they were fed, were given horses, and were allowed to select any woman in the surrounding area that they wished to serve them.

He had made it a policy that when one of his men wanted, they could reject the woman and then select another if they desired. The only stipulation was that if they had children, then the that knight had to make sure his children were fed. He found that his knights seemed comfortable with that arrangement.

He had listened repeatedly to the complaints from some of the serf's village leaders. He had asked if the children were getting fed and if they were he asked what more they wanted. He always provided the village an extra amount of grain and the complaint was quieted.

He was now leaning on his two hands that were resting on the recently finished top wall of Ster Kasteel. It had taken ten years to get the castle built to this point. He was looking down to the river that was crowded by the many merchant vessels going up and down the river. He took note of his tax collection boats approaching and getting paid the tax for passing at this point in their journey. He knew that his larger enforcement boat loaded with young bow armed warriors would catch any boat not willing to pay the tax. They would then demand thirty percent more or they would kill the boat's captain. That had only happened once so far. The word had gone out about the consequence of not paying the tax and the collection had become routine. Some vessels had tried to go past at night to no avail. He had a series of torches continuously burning on the other side of the river and had his tax collectors watching for boats trying to go past at night.

The tax was slowly replenishing his precarious finances and he planned on building a nest egg that would carry him and his family well into the future.

He had strained his finances to have the castle built. He had designed the star shaped twelve-meter-high base and its twelve-meter-deep mote so that a small contingent of knights would be able to defend the castle against almost any army. He hoped that such a situation would never happen.

He had designed two chutes along each star wall where hot burning oil or hot water could be poured down on any attackers that might get to the wall. They would only be able to get there through the arrows and spears that would be continuously raining down on them.

The two entrance gates were two hands thick and six meters high. The wall above it was at the same height as the star walls and had three chutes that allowed hot oil to be poured across the entire entrance.

He had designed living quarters for all of his small contingent of knights. The Knights and their mates were provided with a place to live, food and a small stipend for protecting the castle, cleaning and cooking and doing a variety of the many chores required to keep the castle operational.

He and his family lived in the castle proper that rose seven stories into the sky. He was now standing on the seventh level. There was one more room that rose on the very center tower of the castle above all else. He often sat at this highest level and enjoyed the breeze that came from the west through the openings that provided a circular view of the entire countryside. Those days were few, but all were memorable.

The wall he was standing on went from a circular tower at the base of each star point and formed the highest level which served as the ultimate fighting location in case the castle had somehow been breached.

He had designed a six-by-six-meter water tank close to each tower that was two meters deep. It caught the rainwater. Channels leading from it watered the flower beds at each level and provided drinking water to all levels below. These tanks were normally kept full by the rains. Having the tanks at the seventh level saved a tremendous amount of work. He was sure that they had paid for themselves in the reduction of staff that would have had to carry water up all the flights.

He had also designed a very large water tank at the entrance level that was fed by spring water. He always had one large container of that water at hand wherever he happened to be in the castle. It was one of his self-indulgences.

The raised flower bed around this entrance water tank hid the tank from view. His guests always wondered where he got all his smooth sweet tasting water. He always joked that it became sweet when he dipped his finger into the water from the river.

He was recognized as a shrewd trader in his own rights. He focused his trade on the top tier goods in clothing, exotic fruits and top whiskeys and liqueurs. This did not generate as much income as the taxes, but it was the icing on the cake of a luxurious life.

He had a very lovely wife and had six children with her, which he enjoyed on a daily basis. He also had a few children with several other women who he supported but seldom interacted with.

He enjoyed his life well beyond what he had ever expected.

Knight Gerrit Van Gesterte lived well beyond the normal life expectancy of the year 986 AD. He outlived most of his children, but his line continued for more than three hundred years.

Then a group of roque knights from the Saxony region surprised the unprepared family and took over control of Star Castle. They and their descendants operated Star Castle's still lucrative but declining tax business for another three hundred years. Then they rapidly lost control of the tax collection because the transport vessels increased in size and were able to arm themselves with small cannons. Once that happened the focus turned to the still lucrative import business.

The descendants were able to live off the import business that had grown but it in no way matched the easy money that had been made by collecting taxes. The castle continued to be the dominant force in the area.

Then in fifteen eighty-six the family had to summit to the rule of the Spanish. The table was turned. They were now the ones who had to pay the taxes for the goods they were importing. When one member of the family was hanged for not doing so, the other members made sure to let the authorities know that they were complying.

For the next one hundred fifty years the descends of the rogue knights were ruled by the Spanish branch of the Hapsburgs.

Then around Seventeen forty the Star Castle family once again flourished as they participated in an active trading business and enjoyed the wealth, they were able to generate when The Netherlands became one of the wealthiest and most powerful countries in the world. The family of that period built several ships and were part of the Golden Age of The Netherlands and they were able to once again generate the wealth that would carry them through many years.

The power of the Netherland declined, and the Golden Age ended. However, the Star Castle family had amassed a huge nest egg that would carry them through another two hundred years.

Then the fate of Star Castle became one of decline as it regularly changed owners and a continuous slow decline in its structural integrity seemed to act like the spread of a cancer.

The last family to own Star Castle held on through two World wars. That period saw the family slowly pass on until in early in the twenty-first century only an old couple and one loyal servant remained.

The servant and the husband passed on first and then there was only one. One aging woman who lived alone in a sprawling empty castle. A castle that was now well deteriorated and badly in need of repair.

She was befriended by a seemingly friendly Vajen de Vries. Vajen had her own vision of how to use Star Castle to generate her own wealth and like the roque knights from Saxony who killed the owners of Star Castle she poisoned and killed the person who she thought was the last to own the Castle.

It was a different time and she had to make sure that she was not caught. She was not a sword swinging knight of old, she was a much more devious evil soul that chose to use an undetectable poison.

She had killed the old lady and had not even been suspected of doing so. The coroner had declared the death as heart stoppage due to age. He did not suspect foul play. She had used a poison that after a few hours was undetectable. She had plenty left over. She smiled as she thought about the fact that she had committed the perfect crime.

She stood at almost the same spot as the original builder of the castle, looking out to the small river that made its way towards the sea. She was contemplating how she was going to keep control of Star Castle. She knew what she wanted to do but she did not have the power or the wealth that the original builder had. She had to somehow get the funding to do what she wanted.

She had befriended and then killed the person who she thought was the last remaining owner. The owner was a frail ailing eighty-five-year-old, lonely woman who had come to realize that she could no longer afford to keep and maintain Star Castle. The old lady considered herself royalty but in fact was just the last member of a very wealthy family whose wealth had slowly and steadily decreased.

Vajen had inquired about relatives or other people that might have a claim to the castle. When it seemed that there were no descendants to worry about, she had explored ways to gain control of the castle. She first managed to convince the old lady to give her the power of attorney. Then she began to explore ways to speed her exit into the next world.

She learned about a drug that would induce a heart attack and would be undetectable after a few hours. Once she found the source of it in one of the Eastern bloc countries, she made a special trip to obtain it. Then she slowly gave the old lady enough each day until she had a heart attack. She waited until the next morning to "discover" the old lady's death and then called the police to report the death.

Now she was trying hard to be the one that acquired the castle. She had grown up always hearing from her parents how poor they were and that if it was not for the government providing health care and the child subsistence help, they would all have been dead long ago. She had gone to school always using hand me down clothes that her parents got from their friends.

She had been caught several times shoplifting or stealing sweet goods during her teen years.

She had then concentrated on doing well in school and had entered a trade school that trained her to fill a support role such as a secretary or clerk.

Her shoplifting skills had improved, and she outfitted herself in a few top fashions.

After a few years she transitioned into selling properties where she not only charged the highest commission possible but always included several thousand dollars of additional fees. She became very good at inflating the asking price and thereby getting the top commission.

It was a salary that had put her at the higher end of incomes, but she was not satisfied and was constantly on the search for how to make more.

Star Castle provided her with the opportunity to catapult her to the status of being wealthy.

She had submitted a proposal to the country's Tourism board and highlighted how the castle could be a boon to the area and employ dozens of people. She hope to get them to offer some financial aid. She had also submitted the same information to the department of Historical and Cultural Safeguarding in hopes of getting their approval.

She was currently awaiting for a reply from both. When she got approval, she would go after more finances to make the grounds into to a series of money-making shops, restaurants, and night spots. If she got approval, she was sure she would be able to get that financial support.

She hired a grounds keeper to spruce up the five hundred acres around the castle and to reactivate the flower gardens inside the castle. This would let her point out the improvements she was already making.

She had found the person who she thought was perfect for the job. The person, Aleta, was an ex-legal assistant that wanted to get a job where she was not reporting to a boss that took advantage of her. Vajen identified with this train of thought. She, however, paid her at the bottom end of the pay scale for the kind of work she would be doing knowing that she was taking advantage of the young woman.

She had walked around with Aleta and learned that she had grown up on a vegetable farm bordering a small river in the middle of the Netherlands.

Aleta shared that the castle overlooked a river about the same size as the one she had fished in and boated on. She added that the small village near Star Castle that had only about three thousand inhabitants was almost the same size as the village near her parent's farm.

Vajen looked around the top floor of the castle where she was standing and took in the puffy short purple flowers that bordered taller bright yellow blooming flowers that now were growing in each of the six large flag stone flowerpots. She had also been impressed with the entrance courtyard that now had a stunning red and yellow rose garden trimmed by the same purple flowers all in full bloom.

She had complemented Aleta for having accomplished the transformation while keeping the cost so reasonable.

Aleta had let her know that she had purchased the flowers from one of her father's friends who had given her a special rate. He had even delivered the flowers and helped plant them. It was his expertise and his helper that had made the rapid transformation possible.

Vajen had studied the history of Star Castle and was writing a series of information sheets that she thought she could use when she made the castle a tourist spot.

She imagined the time, some nine hundred years ago, when the first owner had the castle built on a fortified star-shaped base with a deep mote surrounding it. The owner had built the castle so his personal army could hold the castle against any attackers. The star shape was meant to pull the attackers into a position were arrows and spears could be thrown down from two sides to decimate the attackers. He had also set up locations where boiling oil or water could be poured down on the attackers. There was no record of the castle ever being attacked so she did not know if any battles had ever taken place.

The part of the castle that became the living area was built in the center on top of the stare shaped base. It had one round tower located at the base where the actual star shape went out to shape the star point. She thought it had been a genius design. There were a series of independently standing small houses where the servants and other lay persons, who served the lord of the castle and his family, resided.

This first owner of the castle had become exceptionally wealthy by collecting taxes of any commercial vessels traveling the river. That wealth allowed him to virtually be the king of a small portion of what would become the Netherlands.

Much of the stone for building the castle was obtained from the digging of the mote but a huge amount had come from the river. The river water was used to keep the mote filled. But a natural spring brought water up and was delivered to a holding tank that was in the center of the entrance rose garden. This tank had been one of the first things the last owners had kept in good repair. Vajen figured that plumbing could be installed and routed throughout the castle when she had control of it.

She had learned that the castle had stayed with the first owner's family for several hundred years and had continued to keep the family wealthy.

Then in some confrontation a group of German warriors had surprised the folks in the castle by walking in through the open gates and had killed all of its occupants. These warriors used the Castle as their party place, a place to make money by enforcing the taxing of the commerce vessels traveling the river with goods and a place far enough away from their own enemies that it made for a good place to retreat.

During the time of the warriors the partying was legendary and was described in several accounts that talked about the food, the drinking, and the fact that much of the drinking and eating spilled out to the entrance bridge and bones were thrown into the mote. There were also tales of people that were killed in fights being thrown in with chains wrapped around them to keep them down.

Vajen wondered if those stories were true and wondered if the mote was excavated and what would be found.

Then the trade routes had changed, and the river traffic had declined, and the castle lost its importance as a collector of taxes.

During both World Wars the castle had been used by the German army as their headquarters. It proved to be a good location from where they could control the Netherlands.

Vajen was fascinated to learn that much of the German army that had circumvented the famous French Maginot Line had traveled through the Netherlands.

The castle's more recent ownership had changed every few hundred years and the castle had slowly fallen into disrepair.

Vajen envisioned the property being turned into a park. She figured that she would put in food concession stands, a variety of children-oriented venues and a variety of adult venues such as a beer garden, bars that featured entertainment and allowed gambling. She figured she would not have to spend a penny of her own money but would be able to demand a percentage.

She thought the property had great beauty, but it was the thought of making money and making her wealthy that drove her.

She had no idea that what she saw as her path to victory would turn out to be a Pyrrhic Victory.

While she waited for the approval of her proposals she was surprised when a distant cousin, of the old lady, turned up and claimed the ownership of Star Castle. When he met her, he let her know that he was interested in selling the Star Castle and the property. He had no desire to own it.

She had wanted to eliminate him but there was no way to do so and not get caught.

He was currently pushing her to advertise more broadly, and she had complied by putting small advertisements in several newspapers in the US, in South Africa and Brazil. She complied but in a minimalist way.

She continued to try to figure out how she could end up with the castle and the property.

She heard little from any of the advertising and hoped that she would land the support of the local development board before she had to face any competition from overseas.

Then she got a letter from a Lisa Roberts asking about the castle. She delayed the response for several weeks until she got a text from Lisa. She then answered the letter letting her know that the Castle asking price was two point five million dollars. She had pushed the asking price up by a million dollars and hoped that would discourage any additional questions.

All was quiet for a few weeks and then Lisa asked if she and the family could come and get a look at the castle.

There was no way to say no that would not expose her subterfuge. She gave her a date only a few days out hoping that it would be too close for flight reservations. She was disappointed to learn that Lisa agreed and said that the date fit her family's plans.

Figuring out how to discourage Lisa from thinking about buying the castle became the focus of her thinking.

She thought about telling Lisa that there was a huge tax that the government put on foreign buyers.

She thought of hiring some thugs to confront and beat up her and her husband. She was aware of several gangs that would likely be willing to do so if she offered the right incentive.

She figured that perhaps she could use the poison she had used on the old lady on this Lisa.

She remembered the stories about the castle being haunted and decided to resurrect that ghost.

She figured Aleta might fall for that and share it with Lisa. She decided to implement all of her ideas. She was determined to get control of Star Castle. And she was sure she would be able to do so at all cost.

Chapter 2: The Meaning of it All

Lisa held the picture of she, her parents and her younger brother who had died of acute leukemia. The picture had been taken when she was fourteen and her brother was twelve. At the time neither of the two knew that he would be gone in less than a year. They were standing on a dock at Greenwood Lake just before going fishing on a boat her parents had rented. She remembered that her brother, Jason, had caught the biggest fish that anyone in the family had ever caught. They took it home and her mother baked it with its head on. She had the picture of Jason holding the fish when they returned to the dock. It was one of her favorite pictures. It was less than a year later that he was diagnosed with acute leukemia. The needed transfusions became very frequent. She was holding one of his hands and her mother the other when he died in his bed at home. She still recalled the feeling of utter remorse and sadness of that day.

It was devasting to her. Her parents were distraught, but they decided that they would all go back to the lake that Jason had loved because of the fish that he had caught there. She was the one that caught the biggest fish that day. Her mother cooked the exact meal that she had cooked for Jason. The table was set with four plates. She served the meal and made sure Jason had food on his plate. She remembered crying as her father said a prayer wishing a happy life for Jason.

She still though often about her younger years and the wonderful life that she lived. She had grown up in a working middle-class family and by those standard her current lifestyle was a decadent one. Her mother was a legal secretary, and her father was a successful independent plumber. After Jason's death the family seemed to come closer together and every weekend was spent in some short of outing or other family event. During the summer and early fall it was a picnic or a trip camping, water skiing, fishing, and hiking at one of the many parks in New York State. During the winter it was skiing, ice skating, or spending time discussing the current book that they were reading. She had been blessed with great parents. She wished dearly that her brother would have lived to grow up with her.

Her parents were now both retired and still living in the family home where she had grown up. She visited them almost every month. Her daughters were spoiled when they went there and got whatever they wanted. Both Laura and Lillian loved their two grandparents and were always eager to go for a visit.

She figured that perhaps her early life that she had enjoyed so much might be the reason for her current uneasiness.

Her family had shared many wonderful experiences, it was a much simpler life than the one her family was currently living.

She put down the picture of her brother and looked out of the patio through the large six-foot-high surrounding windows, at the family's sixty-two-foot sailing yacht at the end of the pier. She took in the blue waters of South Oyster Bay that divided Long Island from Connecticut. It had a slightly darker color than the clear blue sky that was currently filled with high puffy cumulus clouds. It reminded her of a scene from the movie Soylent Green where the most beautiful scenes where shown to a person just before they died. It all was gorgeous.

She, however, was not standing to enjoy the view, she was contemplating what it all meant. She knew that by all the standards of her peer group she and her family were wealthy. Why then was she not jubilantly happy and why was she thinking that her family needed a change. She smiled at the thought that it was not wealth but great relations that made her happy. She had those great relations and decided that unhappiness was the wrong way to described her current discontent. It was her concern for the future wellbeing of her family that was causing her concern.

She turned and walked back into her living room that had been decorated by a very talented interior decorator and looked very much like a page featured in one of the interior decorator magazines. It was kept immaculately clean by a cleaning crew that came in once a week. This made her family life much easier, but she realized that it was also a symbol of the decadence that was now so concerning to her.

She realized that she had guided her family to practice many of the things her mother had done to make her young life fulfilling. It had just been on a larger and grander and more decadent scale. They snow skied in all the major ski resorts across the country. They had visited many of the National parks where they had camped out but camped out in air-conditioned tents that had viewing windows on the top so you could lie and watch the stars. They had boated and fished but from their sixty-two-foot sailing yacht.

She knew that she had instilled the right philosophy into her two daughters.

Her family was very close so in that respect she had been successful, but she wondered if in the long run she had missed the mark. She wanted to have the family continue to enjoy the atmosphere of respect and love that she sensed they all had. She, however, saw the stress of their success slowly chipping away at that atmosphere.

She and each family member took responsibility to prepare a family dinner each day. But they all had well-paying professional jobs that took up most of their time. So quite often the person whose turn it was to cook would have the dinner delivered. Each of the family had selected several restaurants whose menus provided a good variety, and the meals were always great.

She had cornered the Asian menu with Chinese, Thai and Vietnamese restaurants that delivered great meals. When it was her turn, she would select a variety of items off one of the menus and set up her family dinner.

Craig had captured the Italian menu. He did something similar and though he had kept his focus narrow, his dinners were often the most liked. If you liked Italian food, his dinners were always the best.

Laura had the Indian menu, and her mix was always interesting and quite good. Lisa however was not a fan of the heavy Indian spicing. So, she often ate a log of nan and chicken.

Lillian had the Irish, German, and Spanish menus. She was the one that had the greatest variety of dinners. Her dinners were always great though many of them were on the heavy side and usually required extra time jogging or doing exercise.

Having a good meal was never an issue because all of them had also become accomplished in cooking great meals. Most of the time each of them only cooked one meal per month and the rest was ordered in.

Lisa considered all of them professionally successful.

She was a partner in a very successful law practice. Her office did a booming business and it required much more than a forty-hour work week. She was well compensated and most likely could have provided all the money the family needed.

Craig had a very successful engineering company that had a large multiyear contract with the city of New York. He almost always spent several hours at home each evening doing the prep work for some meeting or other.

Laura, her oldest, had a Master of Engineering degree and was working for her father as one of the lead project engineers. In the evening she was often in conversation with him about some detail about her current project.

Lillian, the youngest, had a Finance degree, and was keeping the books for Craig's consulting firm. Lillian claimed she was working for the best boss she could think of. She did not bring her work home but was often the last to make it to their evening dinner. She had a hectic day almost every day of the week and then closing the books every month really stretched her day and she often went in during the wee hours of the morning.

Lillian claimed she was working for the best boss she could think of.

Lisa tended to agree with Lillian about Craig being a great boss.

Craig was a rock that bonded the family together with his lighthearted attitude that exuded the caring nature that made him loved by his friends and admired by all of his staff.

His business was booming, and he paid his staff well. He had a profit-sharing plan that was generous and basically was a set of golden handcuffs. He was proud of his one hundred percent employee retention rate. He easily took the teasing from them about his being a generous nepotist and had something to tease each of his staff of fifty employees.

He was actively diversifying his customer base to ensure long-term business continuity. He anticipated that at some point he might lose his biggest customer and was acting during the good times to broaden his business service base.

He also insisted that each of his employees participated in some sort of self-enrichment activities of their choosing.

She had attended his company's poolside cookouts and had sailed with him with some of his employees and knew that he had an extremely loyal set of employees.

She envied the environment he had created at his workplace.

She knew that the family was trapped in a golden glove mouse trap. They were maintaining a lifestyle that would never give them their own time to relax and just absorb the beauty of the world around them.

She yearned for a lifestyle that kept the family together but allowed each of them the time and space to enjoy each other and have time with their friends.

She wanted her two daughters to meet someone that would be their soul mates. She wanted them to have the same relationship that she and Craig enjoyed. She was concerned that would never happen if something did not change.

She thought about what type of business they could all share that would give them that space.

The idea of running a lucrative bed and breakfast took shape and she began looking in magazines and newspapers for large homes or suitable buildings in some unique location. She wanted something out of the ordinary that the family could turn into a lifetime project. The search seemed to go on and unsuccessfully on.

She was ready to throw in the towel on that idea when she saw a small three by six-inch advertisement that featured a place in The Netherlands that was referred to as Star Castle. It caught her eye, and she immediately sent a text to the person who had placed the ad. She waited a week waiting for a response and then when she got none she decided to call.

She was surprised to get through. She spoke to Vajen de Vries the realtor and asked about Star Castle. It seemed to her that Vajen was less than anxious to make the sale. She had to ask all the questions about the castle and pull to get the sales price. She was surprised at the asking price of two and a half million dollars. She was not sure what the market price was on a castle.

She knew that she would have to see the property and the castle to know if it was a fair price and if it fit into the category of a family project. The call ended with her asking when she could see the castle.

She was not ready to share her idea of a castle made into a bed and breakfast with her family so instead she suggested a vacation in Amsterdam, The Hague and Rotterdam. It pleased her that the family bought in and even thought the idea of going there in two weeks for a two-week vacation was acceptable.

The two weeks would let her get a firsthand look at the castle to determine if it had the potential to be the project that she thought it might be.

She called Vajen to let her know that she would meet her in two weeks and asked about a place nearby where they could stay. She was informed that the village near the castle was small and perhaps she might consider driving in from a larger city.

Lisa chose to get the telephone numbers of the two small hotels in the village. She wanted to stay close to the castle to get a feel for the surrounding area.

She called her office's support and asked her to arrange round-trip first-class tickets to Amsterdam for the entire family. Normally she would have worked for weeks to get as low of a price for tickets as possible but in this case, she figured it was easier to just have someone else do it.

She smiled about the fact that she was using her wealth to make things easier on herself. Her mother would have labeled her as a wealthy person using wealth as the lever that most people had no access to.

She was not surprised when Craig asked what her real reason was for her to immediately schedule the trip. He pointed out that usually she would ponder a vacation location and spend almost six months figuring out when the best time would be on everyone's schedule and then scout around for the lowest priced tickets. This he pointed out was a very different behavior.

She confessed that she had an ulterior motive. She shared the fact that she was planning to look at a castle that was for sale. She told him she was planning to check it out to see if it had the potential, she hoped it might have.

Craig laughed and asked how much castles were selling for and gave a small whistle when she mentioned two and a half million dollars. He asked what condition the castle was in and what she was planning to do with a castle.

She said that she wanted to get a feel for the condition and if it could be used for the idea she had. She confessed that it might cost another couple of million to refurbish it and get it into the condition necessary to attract paying guests.

Craig shook his head and said that would certainly cause the family some cash flow challenges.

Craig then asked if she was planning to hire someone to manage the castle.

That was when she shared that she was thinking that perhaps it would be a family project and they would be the ones to make the improvements and manage the castle.

He said that he would support her but suggested that she share her idea with the two girls to see if they were interested in such a venture.

She agreed that she would do so on the coming weekend. She added that she wanted to do a little online checking before sharing her idea.

She went online to see what she could find out more about Star Castle. There was a brief description of the castle and a picture that did not show much but the entrance area.

In the ad she found the phone number for the groundskeeper. She wondered why that had been included in the ad but figured that person might give her some additional information.

She placed the call. It was answered in Dutch, and she let the person who answered know that she did not speak Dutch and asked if she spoke English.

The person at the other end switched to an almost perfect US English and introduced herself as Aleta Mulder and asked how she might be of help.

Lisa explained her interest in Star Castle, and the property that came with it and what physical condition the castle was in.

Aleta explained that she was not the person responsible for the sale of the castle and she would get Ms. De Vries to call her back.

Lisa let her know that she had talked to that person, but she wanted to hear from a person that had hands-on experience on the grounds and in the castle.

Aleta was silent for a moment and then she explained that she had started her job as a keeper only a few months before, but she had fallen in love with the castle and with the property it sat on. She shared the fact that she was raised on a vegetable farm, had become what in America was called a legal secretary and after a few years realized that she hated what she was doing. Now she was back doing what she loved.

She then said that for the last six months she had cleaned out much of the wild brush that had started to take over the grounds and she had planted flowers in all of the castle's flower beds. She said she was proud of the change of appearance that she had made on the property and in the castle.

Lisa liked what she heard, and she enjoyed the enthusiasm that Aleta had about the castle and what she was doing. If she bought the property, she would make sure that Aleta would continue to be the groundskeeper.

She thanked Aleta and said that she looked forward to meeting her in person and planned to be there in the next couple of weeks.

On Sunday it was her turn to cook the family dinner meal. On Saturday she went to the grocery and purchased the ingredients that she needed to cook the meal that she had decided on.

She planned on lobster tail and filet mignon, a small bowl of lobster bisque since she figured that there was always room for more lobster. For sides she would have corn on the cob, coleslaw, biscuits, and a green salad. For dessert she would prepare Creme Brule.

She knew which wine she would serve with the dinner and the desert wine that would complement the desert.

Sunday was spent morning getting things ready. She marinated the filet and prepared the lobster tail. She had the sides prepared ahead of the main dish. She then put the four lobster tails into the oven and the filets in her frying pan.

She asked Laura and Lillian to set the table and then got them to help put all the food out.

When they found out what the menu was, they asked if they had missed something and wondered what the special meal was for.

Lisa said that they would find out during dinner.

<u>Chapter 3: The Netherland Vacation</u>

Craig looked at the dinner table where each plate had a thick Filet and Lobster tail, half of a cob of corn and around each plate were sides of coleslaw, soup that he presumed was lobster bisque and a small salad. A glass of water and a glass of dark red wine completed the setting.

He knew then that Lisa was serious about and anxious for everyone to buy into her idea of a bed and breakfast. He shook his head as he thought about the place called Star Castle in The Netherlands. He had sensed that Lisa for some reason had become concerned about the family. He wondered what that concern could be.

He was personally curious about the possibility of a new family venture. He also figured if it happened it would give him a chance to promote one of his top performers by promoting her into the role of CEO in the consulting company. It would let him move onto a new adventure.

He was not sure about the two girls but figured they could make their own decisions. He figured if the adventure materialized, they would most likely be part of it.

After a few bites Laura commented that the Fillet was to die for, and her one bite of lobster was buttery delicious, but she wanted to know whether the dinner was a bribe.

Lillian laughed and said that of course it was and then asked why they were being bribed.

After taking a sip of wine Lisa said that on the upcoming trip to The Netherlands, she was planning to take a look at a castle that she was thinking she might buy.

Laura shook her head and said that she and Lillian had been wondering about what the pile of realty magazines and folded newspapers with circled homes for sale had been all about. They had never imagined a castle in The Netherlands. She added that it made her really curious, and she was looking forward to the trip.

Lillian raised her wine glass and made a toast, "here is to our visit to a castle that Mrs. Roberts wants to buy."

Lisa smiled and said that at the moment she was very interested, but she first had to see the place for herself, and she also wanted the family to agree to the purchase if it came to that. She felt that they should make it happen together as a family.

Lillian asked if what was meant by together as a family was that they would move to The Netherland to convert the castle into a bed and breakfast. The conversion idea had come from the many ads she and Laura had seen that were circled in the many ads they had come across.

Lisa nodded and said that was what she had in mind.

Laura put her fork and knife down and took a sip of her wine. She then said that it all sounded a bit crazy and a little farfetched. They knew no one in The Netherlands. The few friends they had were in New York or somewhere in the states. She added that she had just made a new friend and was not sure she would want to move to the Netherlands.

Craig suggested that they wait until they all got to see this castle and then discuss the likelihood of agreeing with his dear wife's potential delusion and then they could decide whether she needed counseling.

He raised his glass and made a toast to a fun vacation and the adventure at the ghost haunted Star Castle.

After the toast Lillian asked if the castle was really haunted.

Craig nodded and replied that the castle had been built in nine hundred AD and he was sure that in a thousand years it had accumulated many ghosts.

The next two weeks were a flurry of getting their work organized for their two-week absence.

When they understood the planned itinerary, Laura and Lillian said that they thought that visiting The Hague, Rotterdam and the Castle was too much and suggested to skip from Amsterdam to the Castle and spend more time there.

Lisa was happy about how the family was supporting her wild idea about the castle and agreed that putting more time into visiting the castle was the most practical thing to do. It would give them more the time to explore the area around the castle to determine what other attractions there might be. She was feeling fairly bullish about her idea.

A few days later, after a short trip to LaGuardia they were sitting in the lounge discussing what they would do on their vacation until the boarding call.

After boarding and finding her seat, Lillian commented that she was planning to enjoy the flight as she sat down. She tried out the controls and lay flat.

Laura smiled and said that she was planning to get as much sleep as possible because she wanted to be fresh and ready for the tour of Amsterdam.

Lisa let them know that she had planned an active Amsterdam stay. Each day had one specific focus. Each day started out with breakfast at the hotel, then they would go to the first attraction and afterwards dinner.

The first day was an outdoor concert at Vondelpark. She said that she was not sure what would be played so it would be a surprise. Afterward they would take a casual walk in the park followed by dinner at a nearby restaurant. She said that would give them a nice slow but active start.

Craig commented that after flying there a slow start sounded like what he would want.

On the second day she had scheduled a visit to the fine arts Rijsksmueseum. The museum featured art pieces of all major Dutch artists and many of the other famous European painters. This she announced was some interesting art education to ground them in the arts and meant to broaden their perspective.

Craig said that he hoped they would have lots of benches where he could educate his achter. He added that if they did not know what that meant in Dutch, they should educate themselves while he broadened his perspective.

Lisa said the third day was special in that they would visit the Anne Frank house. They then would follow that up with visiting the Keukenhof where they would view garden displays of tulips. She expected each of them to walk out with a bag of tulip bulbs to be brought home. They would plant a flower bed to honor Anne.

She smiled when she shared that on the fourth day, they would take a tour labeled the Hieneken Experience. They would take their time and spend the day drinking Hieneken, snacking, learning how the beer was made and then tasting all the different beers that the company made. There was a restaurant associated with the tour that was close by where they would finish the day. She joked that this was their day of debauchery.

On the fifth day they would go to the Royal palace that was huge, and they would likely walk for miles. This was intended to make them realize they were humble serfs and to make them appreciate the next day.

The next day they would take a boat tour of the city on a private boat. She smiled and said that this was a recovery day so they would be ready for a full day of shopping that was to follow. She shared that she had talked with the captain of the boat and found him very interesting, and she was looking forward to his tour.

She said that she had saved the last day for shopping on De 9 Straatjes, which was a shopping area where they would spend the entire day walking from shop to shop. She had reservations for lunch then afterwards they would shop some more.

Dinner would be at a restaurant specializing in Dutch cuisine where they would be able to select from a wide variety of traditional dishes.

After landing at Schiphol airport in Amsterdam, getting their luggage and then riding in the taxi for about forty-five minutes, they arrived at the hotel.

Laura asked if the reservations had been purposely made at a hotel that flew the multicolored Gilbert Pride flag.

Lisa said that she had made reservations at this particular hotel because it was central to what she was planning, and they featured a great breakfast. She said that she recognized the flag and knew what it meant but that had not been on her mind when making the reservations.

Laura laughed and said the tour was already interesting and it made her look forward to the rest of the week.

The days went by in rapid fire. They all agreed that having the evenings free left enough room for each of them to relax.

Laura and Lillian went out on two of the evenings to local pubs and enjoyed the social scene. They agreed that they liked the Dutch atmosphere that they had so far experienced in Amsterdam. It was interesting and the local people seemed to be super friendly. They agreed that it was the opposite feeling when they went out in New York where things seemed to move at a very fast pace and the crowd was more interested in their personal groups.

On their fifth day they all agreed that they were ready to take the boat tour and just relax. The boat was a work of art. The boat hull was a dark brown highly varnished wood. The front half had a roof cover that was made of a lighter brown wood. It had long windows along the side and the interior had light tan leather couch-like seats on each side. The back half where their seats were located was open and had dark brown leather covered cushioned seats all around. A raised table in the central area held an impressive variety of cheeses, sausage, bread, and a variety of fruit. They all commented on the snacks, and each took one.

The captain welcomed them on board, introduced himself and explained how he would show them all the highlights as they went past them. He said they should ask all the questions that came to mind, and he would see that they got an answer. He joked that he might not give them the right one, but he figured they would never remember what he had said by the time they all got to the end of the tour.

The captain then asked what they would like to drink and offered beer, wine, or soft drinks. Each of them ordered either wine or a beer.

The tour then began, and the boat captain explained the history of the buildings that they passed as they went along the canal. He pointed out the dates that were on the houses. He added that in historic times there were no street signs, and the names of the houses were how folks found their way around.

He explained that the many of the boats tied along the canals were clearly meant to be lived in but were usually weekend or vacation homes.

The boat they were on gave Lisa the idea about having a boat tour associated with the Star Castle bed and breakfast. She asked the boat captain if he was interested in such a venture. He replied that his family was now a part of Amsterdam, and he was not interested but he said he had the business cards of three young boatmen that might be interested. He got her the cards. As he handed them to her, he said she should look carefully at the names. She did and figured out that one of the cards must be his son's card. She put all three in her purse.

At the end of the boat tour, they walked back to the hotel. She reminded everyone that this was the evening she had reservations to a restaurant that boasted the largest selection of traditional Dutch cuisine.

A short time later they met in the lobby and walked to the restaurant.

Once they were seated, she suggested that they each order a different dish and share it with each other. The waitress smiled and offered to bring out each plate with a mix of the most popular traditional Dutch mains and she would bring out the sides so each person would have three sides. She suggested a bowel of Steamed Mussel and a large Dutch shrimp cocktail for the table that could also be shared. She suggested that the Dutch desert Coupe Zanaantje would be an excellent way to finish the dinner. She explained that the desert was vanilla ice cream, warm cherries with a whipped cream topping.

They all agreed that it sounded great and that it would be more than they could possibly eat but they were going to try.

And try they did. The table conversation was about how great everything was and how great the vacation had been so far.

As they left the restaurant, Lillian said she was glad that it was a long walk back to the hotel. She added that just the dinner made the trip worthwhile.

Laura nodded and added that the last few days had been one of the better family vacations. She hoped that it would continue to stay in that category.

The shopping the next day exhausted all of them. It seemed like a continuous walk.

Craig was not into shopping and often sat at the entrance of a shop watching the tourists as well as the locals going by. As they walked, he was enjoying the constant discussion about fashion that went on between the three women.

He was pulled into one shop where the three insisted that he buy a grey shirt and a pair of trousers. They insisted it made him look dashing.

He was happy when the shopping spree ended, and they were ready to finish the day trying one last restaurant in Amsterdam.

The following morning, they loaded all their suitcases into the back of a van. The van had six comfortable seats in the back with a small table between the last two rows of seats. The side windows curved over the top of the van and provided a great view.

The driver pointed out the cooler with snacks and a variety of drinks. He informed them that the drive would take close to two hours and that he would point out several sites that they would pass on the drive to Star Castle. He added that the scenery was beautiful but there were few tourist stops.

Lillian replied that for the moment she was toured out and would just enjoy the scenery and the ride.

The driver thanked Lisa for hiring him for the week and promised that he would make sure that he was at their disposal at all times of the day. After giving Lisa his card, he asked that everyone put on their seat belts, and they took off.

During the drive, Lisa reviewed her notes and commented that the realtor did not seem to want to sell the castle. She shared that the grounds keeper whose name was Aleta had provided a wonderful and enticing description of the property and the castle that had convinced her to make the trip. She said that she hoped the description of the place was at least half of what had been shared.

<u>Chapter 4: Aleta</u>

Aleta had come home to let her parents know that she was taking a job as a groundskeeper. She planned to do that during the Sunday dinner. She was not sure how her parents would take it. They had both been happy when she landed a job as a legal secretary. She wondered what the reaction was going to be this time.

They had all walked to the river and were fishing in a small alcove. She was thinking about her decision as she watched the fishing bobber slowly move toward her. She smiled as she realized she had a fish on her line. She quietly let her mother and father know that she had one.

Her mother smiled and said that she hoped it was big enough for all of them since so far no one had caught any fish.

The dinner that evening consisted of a large baked fish surrounded by cut carrots, small potatoes cut in half and broccoli heads soaked in melted butter.

Her mother commented that the entire dinner was prepared with the food that they had raised.

They had one milk cow, several sheep and one large sow that provided a yearly litter. The litter was raised until they were large enough to sell. The local butcher usually bought the lot and gave one half of one of them back.

The dinner discussion centered on whether she had yet found a nice young man and how was work going.

Aleta figured it was as good a time as any to share that she had just accepted the role of groundskeeper of Star Mote Castle.

Her father smiled and commented that it sounded like a lot of work. He asked why she was leaving what he thought was a very good job for one that would have her doing hard outdoor labor.

Aleta replied that it was his fault because he had raised her working in all of their vegetable and flower gardens. She said that working in an office at first seemed like a good job, but she soon realized that it bored her, and she yearned to work outdoors. She said that she had searched for such a job and found that such jobs were few and far between. She could have become a small package deliverer using a bicycle, but she knew that that was not a job that she thought she could last very long doing. She wanted to get a job that would last her a lifetime.

She confessed that the pay she had accepted to get the role of Star Castle groundskeeper was two thirds of her current salary but when she walked the grounds around Star Castle and had gone inside of it, she knew that the job was what she wanted.

She had negotiated the right to use one of the small workhouses inside the castle free of charge. She said that what she would save on rent, made up for her reduced salary.

Her father asked if he could go with her to get a look at where she would be living.

Her mother insisted that she was going as well and asked what Aleta needed to set up the house in the castle.

Aleta smiled and said that it would be great to have them take her to the castle. She said that the small moving truck was delivering her few possessions on Monday afternoon.

Her mother asked about what would be delivered.

Aleta went down the list of the few things that she owned.

Her mother said that it sounded somewhat meager to set up a new home and they would need to make a list of what else she would have to get. She said for sure they were going to bring an ample supply of the vegetables from the garden. She said that there was enough time to plant a garden and that should happen as soon as they got there.

Her father agreed that getting a garden in would ease his mind.

Aleta smiled as she accepted their suggestions. It was becoming clear to her that she had made the right decision. She had expected a different reaction from her parents but should have known that she would get this kind of support. She hoped her brother, Daan, would also be as supportive.

She suggested that her father bring the fishing poles since the Meuse River ran by the castle and was the water that filled the mote.

She said that she was not sure whether there were any fish in the mote, but they could find out.

When she got out to the pickup truck early Monday morning, she was surprised to find that her brother was there and said that he was going with them. He added that he would ride in the back and make sure the fishing poles would not fall out because he wanted to fish in the mote of a real castle.

Aleta gave him a hug and said that she was happy that he was coming along and that he could make sure that she had taken the right job.

The drive took most of the morning and they arrived at lunchtime. Her father found his way to a road along the river and randomly chose a restaurant.

They walked into the small corner restaurant that had tables outside. They chose an outside table that faced the river and provided a great view of the few boats that were out.

Aleta called her mover and found out that the truck had just arrived and after lunch they would be out to the castle.

She felt good as she sat and enjoyed lunch. Her family was with her, and she was going to be working at something she felt she would love. It seemed that everything was coming together.

They arrived at the Castle and drove up to the massive gate.

The moving truck arrived almost at the same time.

She had the key to the small entrance door to the right side of the gate and unlocked it.

The controls for the large gate were mounted on the inside wall to the left of the small entrance door.

Her father activated the motor to open the large door but almost immediately the breaker popped, and nothing happened.

Her father went out and examined the rollers on the guide rail and the mechanism that pulled the doors open. He said that it would take him most of the day to get everything in working order.

Aleta thanked him for volunteering to fix it but suggested that he spend his time fishing and let the repairs be arranged by whoever bought the castle.

The mover asked where the things in his truck needed to go. He said that everything he had could go through the small door. It took him less than an hour to get everything put into the small cottage that was located to the right side of the castle entrance. She explained that in past times the cottage had been used by the knight that controlled that specific star point.

Her father pointed out that there was no electricity to the cottage.

Aleta realized that she had missed that fact. She needed it for her small countertop oven in which she cooked most of her meals. Her two element cook top was the other thing she critically needed electricity for. She then realized that she had floor lamps and her television that would need it.

She was a little disappointed in the fact she had overlooked such a critical element.

Her father located an exterior electrical power plug out by the circular garden. then said he could set her up with an extension cord but that she would need someone to come in and locate the main electrical panel and see what it would take to get electricity to the cottage.

Aleta took a few moments and found an electrician located in the village and arranged for him to come out and determine what it would cost to run electricity to the cottage.

She then suggested a walk around the outside of the castle and then a quick tour of the inside.

The sun was now getting close to setting. She knew that her parents planned to return home, so she suggested that they try their hand at fishing in the mote before they left.

They were standing on the bridge fishing when both her brother and her mother caught a fish. Both fish were as long as her forearm.

She was glad that there were fish in the mote.

Her mother suggested that she take home one fish and leave one for her to bake in her small oven.

Her brother cleaned both fish and cut the head off the one she was going to keep. She had her metal platter for her oven and the headless fish was a perfect fit.

Her mother gave her a hug and said that she thought the new job was a perfect fit for what Aleta wanted.

She then handed Aleta a bag filled with all the food she had packed. The only thing she was taking back was the fish she had caught.

Her father said the he would keep in touch to see how he could help. He took out two fishing poles and his tackle box and gave it to her brother and said that it should stay until Aleta had her own tackle.

Her brother said he was staying and expected to eat half of the fish he had caught.

Aleta gave him a hug and thanked him for staying. She had been worried how she would handle her first time alone in the castle. On this first night she was worried about the electrical situation.

Her father had left one extra extension cord that had more than one plugin but when she had the little oven plugged in the floor lamp had to be moved close to the cooking area and the rest of the living area was without any direct light.

She prepared the fish and potatoes, made a small salad for the two of them and went out to the clear water pool in the center of the entrance circle and got a pitcher of drinking water. When the fish was done, she moved the floor lamp to where the table was and set everything up for dinner.

The cool of the evening blew in through the windowless cottage openings. It added to the evil threat each dark corner seemed to emote.

She was glad her brother had stayed with her. She added getting windows installed to the growing list of items she would need to get done to make the cottage habitable. She now had electrification, some plumbing work, window work and she wanted a real lock on the door to the cottage.

The next morning the Electrician arrived and gave her an estimate for getting electricity to the cottage and separately getting the interior electrical lines installed. He asked about the number of lights and outlets that she desired.

She asked for his recommendation, and he suggested two outlets on each wall and ceiling lights in the kitchen, entry area, one in the small side room and two in the main area. Once that was determined he handed her the estimate for the work.

She was surprised at the amount, asked if she could get a time payment plan. When she learned that there was a time payment plan, she decided to get the work done immediately.

She was pleased the window company was able to send a person out to show her the available selection and then give her an estimate. She chose the windows that were locally stocked and could be put in during the week. She also used their time payment plan.

The plumber came in and located the hook up for the toilet, future shower, and sink drains. He did not have a time payment plan, so Aleta chose to only have the drain for the sink and the toilet put in.

She added the shower stall to the list of things she would have to save for.

The final immediate project was to get a locksmith out to provide a key to the lock that was on the door and to put in a dead bolt lock on the inside. She also asked him to fix the lock that was on the main door of the Castle. He too did not offer a time payment plan.

When she looked at what she thought was her current available cash she realized she was down to an amount that she would need to nurse carefully until her first paycheck.

At the end of the week, she went to the village and bought a slab of ribs that she planned to grill for a departure lunch.

Her mother had called to let her know that she was bringing down a variety of dry goods that would last Aleta for about a month.

She also said she was bringing a several cooked dishes that would go well with the ribs.

She added that her father was bringing down an entire garden that he had prepared and planned to plant that afternoon around the entrance central tank. He was also bringing enough flowers to make a border around the garden so there would be no complaints about having a garden at the entrance.

They were planning to arrive at noon and would bring pizza for a quick lunch and then they could all help in getting the garden planted.

She added that she hoped to get a little fishing in before leaving to go home.

Daan laughed when he heard what was coming down. He said that their mother was not going to let any of them go hungry. He said that he was constantly asked over for dinner and usually agreed because it saved him a ton of money because when he was on his own, he usually chose to eat out.

Aleta said that having her bring down a ton of stuff would provide the cushion she needed to tide her over until she got her first paycheck.

Daan asked if it was time to go fishing?

Aleta said that she thought they should get the garden area ready first so that when their parents arrived, they could concentrate on planting and watering.

She got an old square and a rigging hoe that she had found in one of the sheds and led the way to the round water trough in the entrance garden. It took them several hours to prepare three rows around the trough and one row a few centimeters from the stone wall that formed the outer part of the center structure.

When it was done Aleta said it was time to go fishing.

She took a large bucket filled with water, the poles, and the worms she had captured when they prepared the garden.

They both had landed several nice fish when they saw the pickup truck driving toward them.

Daan waved and commented that it was time to put the poles away and get ready to go back to work.

Aleta nodded and agreed. She added that she planned to cook the ribs over an open fire using a deep square dish that she would cover with a pizza pan. She said that she had wrapped the marinated, honey covered ribs in aluminum and would let them cook for the next two hours.

This would let them work on planting and watering the garden.

Her father got out of the truck and said that they should first unload all the food that her dear mother had insisted he bring down. He then took out a new fishing pole, tackle box and handed it to Aleta and said that he wanted his poles and tackle box back so that he could go fishing.

Aleta gave him a hug and thanked him. She took the pole and tackle box and carried it in and put it just inside of the door. She figured she would put up two pegs on the wall where she would put the pole. There was a wood storage space next to the old fireplace were the tackle box could easily be kept.

Her mother supervised the unloading of the dry goods and took the tackle box out of the wood storage area and organized her dry goods there. She pointed out the tackle box should go wherever the fishing pole ended up.

She then got everyone to help in bringing in the cooked food. The she arranged it in the kitchen area.

The she said everyone should get out and plant the garden.

Aleta stood back and marveled at the neatly planted and watered vegetable garden and watched as Daan and her father finished planting the row of low lavender flowers around the outside wall.

She went to the water tank and filled her watering can and began watering.

Her father took the can from her and suggested that she join her mother to get the dinner ready. He said that he and Daan would finish the watering and the wash up and come in to eat.

Aleta went in and suggested that they move the table outside and enjoy the late afternoon. She and her mother carried out the table and chairs and Aleta found her one tablecloth and put it on the table.

Her father went out to his truck and returned with two bottles of his home-made wine. He had a dark red wine that was sweet with a taste of the apple that he added to it.

It was a wine that Aleta loved. She knew he had many varieties to chose from and he had chosen one that she was especially fond of.

The meat on the ribs fell off on its own. Her mother praised her for the flavor that they had.

Her father laughed and said that the ribs were great and asked for another helping.

The dinner was one that Aleta was sure she would remember for a long time.

After cleaning up and getting the table back into the house, they all went out to the pickup and after hugs and kisses she watched as Daan, and her parents drove away.

She looked out to where the large red sun was setting. She stood for some time thinking through what had been accomplished over the week. She had windows, a working toilet, water to the sink, a lock on both the castle entrance door and her cottage door and the cottage was wired. She could watch television if she had any local service, but she seldom watched so it would be no issue if she had no reception.

This would be her first day alone in the Castle. She knew she would be comfortable in her new home.
She turned and entered the castle.

Chapter 5: Personal Malus

The drive to the castle followed the small winding Waal River that was bordered on both sides by small thriving farms. The tree lined river seemed to have a wide variety of commercial as well as recreational boats going in both directions. It was a surprisingly busy river. The commercial boats were small versions of the ships that were in the harbors along the coast.

Craig commented that it seemed to be an area that was much less dense than that around Amsterdam but thriving and added that the farms were very well kept and seemed to grow a variety of crops. He pointed out a herd of cows and commented that every farm seemed to have a small herd of milk cows and wondered where all the milk went.

The driver commented that they were driving through the region that was known for the variety of vegetables, cheeses, butter, and the quantity of milk they produced. He added that he thought the area produced almost a third of the dairy products in the Netherlands.

Laura said that the river seemed rather small and was surprised that it had once been a major trade route.

Lillian commented that the boats traveling the river during the height of the castle's existence were much smaller and either powered by sail or by long poles being used by the deck hands to propel and guide the boats.

When they passed a sign with the words Star Castle and an arrow pointing to the left Lisa declared they would soon see if the trip was worth making.

The drive up to the castle was in the shadow between two rows of large, towering oaks. The gravel drive appeared to have been recently cut and each tree had black mulch around its base. The driver stopped the van in the castle's small, shaded parking lot and they all got out.

Lisa stepped out and looked around.

Lillian looked up at the Castle and let out a whistle. She then commented on its size and its grand look.

Craig put his arm around Lisa and asked her if she was as impressed as he was and said that it looked in pretty good shape.

Laura asked if they were going to go in.

Lisa said she would call the realtor to see when they could get a tour. She said that she was surprised at what she thought was a rather cool reception she had so far experienced. Her call was promptly answered, and she was told that the groundskeeper would open the small entrance doorway and give Lisa a tour. Then in the morning they could meet and take a formal tour and discuss the details associated with the purchase of the castle.

Lisa led the way toward the Castle. As they crossed the bridge over the mote the small door to the right of the main castle gate opened and a very attractive blond-haired, blue-eyed woman in work coveralls opened the door and greeted them.

She introduced herself as Aleta and said she was the Star Castle groundskeeper.

Lisa introduced herself as the person who had talked with her over the phone and then introduced everyone else.

Aleta shook hands with everyone, then said that she had been instructed to show them around. She asked what they wanted to see.

Lisa said she wanted to get a quick look around so she could get a feel for the place and what might need to be repaired. She added that she would like to get a walk around the property as well.

Aleta smiled and said that she understood the request, but a tour of the castle would take more than the rest of the day. There would not be enough time to see it all. She added that it would take several days to get a detailed tour of the castle. She said that she had a golf cart that would make a tour of the grounds in a day possible.

Lillian pointed at the yellow rose garden in the entrance center courtyard and asked if Aleta had planted it.

Aleta nodded and added that the water fountain in the middle of the flower bed was a natural spring water fountain that was the only water source for the castle. She added that she used the fountain water to water the flower bed on the first level, but each tower had a tank that captured rainwater in large holding tanks that graced each of the seven levels of the Star Mote Castle. Those tanks provided the plants with water at those levels.

Laura asked how many groundkeepers there were.

Aleta smiled and replied that they were looking at the ground keeping crew.

Craig asked if she had mowed the grass on the driveway in and spread the mulch around the base of each tree.

Aleta gave a small bow and said the first things she had done. She had also ordered in new gravel and had spread it from the highway all the way into the parking lot.

She then said that she would take them up the one tower that she said had one of the best views of the surrounding area. She explained that at each level the wall of the castle connected all the towers together. The walkways at the levels below the seventh level were on the inside and there were slotted windows that were used by bowmen to defend the castle.

When they got to the seventh level, she pointed out the large water filled square stone tank at the base of each tower beneath the roof and said that rain was the source of the water that kept the tanks full. The very top walkway was in the open and there were a series of flower beds along the walls of the walkway.

Aleta pointed out the small troughs along the wall that guided the water from the tank to each of the flowerbeds. She demonstrated how by raising a small wooden board she could let the water in the tank flow to each flower bed. This was the water she used to water the plants at this top level. She added that the pools needed yearly cleaning but so far, she had only cleaned this one. They also each sported some rather large and tasty fish that she caught and ate.

Craig gave a small laugh and commented that she would need to take the family fishing.

Aleta nodded and pointed to a bamboo fishing pole laying by the edge of the pool and said they would need to bring their own fishing poles because she only had one as this level and she kept her reel fishing pole at the cottage, and she used it to go fishing in the mote.

Lisa stood with her hands on the wall and looked out at the river below. She did not know that she was standing in almost the exact spot that Knight Gerrit Van Gesterte, the original builder, had stood in more than a thousand years before as she looked down at the river and the grounds. She sensed the presence of one of the ghosts that Craig had assured everyone would be present in the castle. The scene seemed to flow to the far horizon where the earth seemed to blend with the sky. She was personally very impressed and feeling like she had found what she was looking for. She wondered why it was still on the market.

Craig stood beside her and commented on the grand view. He said that so far, he was very impressed by what he saw, and the castle was not the ruins he had imagined. It clearly needed a ton of work, but it seemed to be very doable.

Laura heard the conversation and added that she too was impressed.

Lillian asked Aleta what her assessment of the structural integrity of the castle was.

Aleta said that almost all the structure needed to be addressed and that there was a ton of work to be done. She said that she had fixed all the flowerpots on her own and figured it would take a significant amount of work to address all the weaknesses that she had seen around the castle.

She added that she had paid one of her father's friend who was a stone mason to fix the water tank at the entrance of the castle.

She pointed out that even the front gate had needed repair so that it would slide to the side smoothly.

She said that she had spent a tremendous amount of time on the grounds and had so far removed more than forty large loads of brush.

Lisa complemented Aleta for making the castle presentable. She asked what Vajen had instructed her to do.

Aleta replied that she had been instructed to make the place look better but all the details she was describing were what she had determined was the priority that she had set for herself.

She added that she had been a legal secretary before and hated her job. She had grown up on a vegetable and flower farm and loved the outdoors. Her mother, father and several of their friends had come to the castle and provided her guidance on how to attack the mess that the castle was in.

Those things that she had needed for herself she paid for. The things she determined were the responsibility of the owner she got Vajen to pay for, or it did not get done.

Lillian said that it seemed that she had done well.

They were still standing at the top wall looking at the scenery as the sun came down to the far horizon and began to turn the clouds in the sky into purple, pink and red colors.

Lisa said that she was in love with the place. She let Aleta know that on the following day she would like to spend the day seeing the grounds around the castle.

Aleta nodded and said she would have the golf cart that she had found on a shed out on the property that her father had resurrected ready to go.

After Lisa and the family left Aleta called Vajen to let her know that the Roberts family seemed to like the property and seemed serious about buying it.

Vajen listened to Aleta say that the family had stayed for most of the day and that Aleta had taken them up the tower that gave the best view of the river and they were all very impressed and that they were planning to return the next day and tour the grounds. Aleta repeated that the family all seemed to really like what they had seen. She said that the person who introduced herself as Lisa seemed to be the one that was the most interested in all the details and had asked about the structural condition of the castle.

After hanging up, Vajen thought about what she should do. She was still waiting to hear back from the development council about her proposal to take over the castle. She decided that she had to take both physical action against Lisa and her family and she would continue the haunting of the castle. Perhaps the combination would make the purchase less attractive.

She had already searched out and talked to a street gang in The Hague and had let them know she had an intimidation job for them. She now gave them a call and arranged for them to come to Star Castle. She intended to use them to discourage Lisa from buying the castle.

After leaving the castle, Lisa suggested they check into their hotel and then plan to go out to dinner. She listened to Laura and Lillian chatting about how charming Star Castle was and how they were looking forward to seeing the grounds.

Craig wondered why the castle was still on the market.

Lisa nodded and then added that she thought perhaps the repair and upkeep costs might be a factor, but she also wondered why the sales agent was taking such a low-key approach to selling it.

When they were checking in, she asked for a recommendation for an evening meal within walking distance.

The next morning, they arrived at the Star Castle grounds at nine.

Aleta drove up in a large open golf cart with cushioned yellow seats. After greetings, they all sat back as Aleta explained that she would first go around the outer perimeter of the property. She said that the distance around was close to four kilometers. She pointed to specific trees and commented that the larger trees currently on the property were all older than three hundred years. The wide-open green areas were kept in a wilder condition. The flowers were a variety of wildflowers that she had seeded that were native to the country. The field was the home of a few deer, pheasants, foxes, rabbits, and a host of smaller animals. She commented that she often sat in her work cart watching the movement of various animals.

She then turned toward the castle and began a much smaller loop about ten meters from the point of the Star.

She stopped the cart and pointed to two pairs of black swans and said that she felt the castle was very lucky to have the two pairs. She pointed to the three young cygnets riding on their mother's back and three more that were scampering around in the water as they chased small fish. She let them know that black swans were only found in the south of The Netherlands.

She then pointed to the castle walls and said that the stones in the walls of the castle most likely needed some serious grouting.

Lisa looked at the wall and asked if Aleta knew of any specific part of the castle that was worse than other places.

Aleta replied that she could point out several places that looked worse than the rest of the castle.

She then continued the tour and pointed out several locations close to the water line where several stones seemed to be coming loose. She said that she had tried to move one stone back into place, but she was not strong enough to do it.

Craig looked at the area that Levi had pointed out and said that scaffolding would need to be put up in the mote itself. He asked how deep the mote was and if there was much mud on the bottom.

Aleta commented that the current water depth was about two meters, and the bottom was filled with mud, but she did not know how deep that was, but said she had been able to push a pole at least two meters down into it.

Laura said that she knew that most motes had an average depth of ten feet. She added that they would have to find out whether they needed to remove the mud from the mote before they began any work on the exterior.

They finished the tour of the land surrounding the castle and decided that they should sit in the courtyard and discuss their assessment of what they had learned so far.

Lillian was standing on the stone wall of the yellow roses. She commented that there seemed to be a garden on the other side of the roses.

Aleta smiled and said that it was her personal tomato, potato, green pepper, eggplant, and okra garden. She added that it was what allowed her to spend her meager income on getting things fixed that she needed to live there.

She asked if they might be interested in ordering in an early dinner. She said that she had several local restaurants that would deliver pizza, Italian spaghetti dishes or a version of Spanish Paella that had clams but only a few shrimp.

Lisa asked what Aleta recommended.

Aleta said that Pizza would be the easiest to manage and probably the fastest to get delivered.

Lisa replied that the pizza sounded good. Everyone else agreed and gathered around Aleta as she phoned in her order. Craig handed her his credit card to pay for it.

Lisa then asked if she could get a look inside each tower while they waited for the delivery.

She asked where Aleta stayed.

Aleta pointed to a small structure and commented that she had set up her room in one of the rooms in what had once been the living area of one of the castle's many knights. There were probably about forty such buildings that were in various states of disrepair. She had picked the one that was closest to the gate. It was one of the ones in better condition.

She led the way to the small house-like structure.

The family followed.

Craig commented that refurbishing these smaller stand-alone units might provide a quick way for improvement to begin. They in turn could provide a place for additional workers to reside.

Lillian said that she thought she would like to live in one of the units.

Laura nodded and said that she could see how it would be a quick way begin the castle improvement and to get a place for them to live in the castle.

She asked who had done the work on Aleta's cottage.

Aleta said the all the materials were local. Local small companies had done the installation of the windows, the counter, and the plumbing. She would be glad to let them look at all the paperwork.

Lisa didn't say anything, but the conversation was a positive indication to her that her family was getting hooked on her vision of making a lifestyle change.

The pizza arrived and they all sat along the wall around the rose garden talking about what they could do with the castle.

<u>Chapter 6: Connection</u>

The night was dark as Vajen crossed the mote. She was dressed in a flowing white lace dress beneath her black cape. This was her fourth haunting. She had asked Aleta whether there was anything unusual happening at the castle and was surprised that Aleta had not seen her going through the castle. This evening she had brought a sound system to provide some haunting music background. She hoped to scare Aleta.

Aleta was standing in the dark watching as the boat crossed the mote. She was almost sure who was pretending to be the castle ghost and was very curious why she was trying to resurrect the story of the Star Castle ghost. She almost gave her position away when the music was turned on. She had to keep herself from laughing. It was the music often used when ghosts were shown in the movies. She decided if on the next day she was asked by Vajen if there was anything unusual happening in the castle, she would say that she thought she had seen a ghost. The question if asked would verify that Vajen was for some reason trying to resurrect the castle ghost.

The next morning Vajen traveled to The Hague where she met with the gang leader she was acquainted with and arranged for him to rough up Lisa and her husband. She let him know that she would let him know who and where to assault the persons she wanted roughed up. She wanted Lisa to be scared about having gangs around the castle and what that might mean for any tourists renting rooms. She wanted to discourage Lisa so she would not want to make the purchase of the castle.

After making the arrangements she drove back to Star Castle. She had arranged to meet Lisa in the afternoon. She planned to point out all the work the Castle needed in hopes of discouraging her from wanting to purchase Star Castle. She hoped that Lisa was stretching her finances to even consider buying the castle. She hoped by highlighting the cost of doing anything with it Lisa would walk away.

Lisa had prepared the family for the meeting with Vajen and said that they should treat her as a potential adversary.

Craig had volunteered that one of his best engineers in the company was from the Netherlands and seemed to know quite a bit about the regulations about the sale of land to foreigners. He said that for something like the castle which would be considered a heritage buy the department of Historical and Cultural Safeguarding would most likely be the controlling body. He had sent over the address and the phone numbers for that department.

Lisa had immediately sent her improvement proposal to the board and sent a request for a meeting to share her vision of how she planned to make improvements to the castle and how her project would boost the local economy.

She emphasized her goal of maintaining the historical integrity of the of the property and Star Castle.

She had asked the family what else was needed to enroll each of them.

Both Laura and Lillian said they needed to get out and experience the nightlife to see if there was anything that attracted them.

Crag let her know that he would support her decision no matter what, but the two girls should decide based on how they felt about the area.

Lisa said that was fair.

Vajen greeted them in the parking lot and after greeting them she led the way to the Castle.

She said that she understood that they had already met Aleta as she opened the gate to Star Castle and then led the way in.

She asked about their initial visit and asked what else would help them to make a decision.

Lisa took the lead and said that she needed to spend at least a few days to see what was needed to refurbish the castle and she wanted to learn about the surrounding area.

Vajen said she could show her all the current problems that she was aware of and emphasized that there were many but added that she was not an architect or engineer and was not sure what was significant in terms of what the priority would be.

Lisa said the she and Craig would be the ones that would accompany her on the tour.

She looked at Lillian and Laura and suggested they corner Aleta and find out about the nightlife in the area.

Aleta smiled when she heard Lisa putting her in charge of sharing the nightlife of the area. Her nightlife was usually spent in her servant's living area or sitting in the golf cart in the early evening watching the animals browsing in the field.

She had made several friends and knew a couple of hard-working young men who she enjoyed having a brew on a Friday or Saturday night and one of them was her current boyfriend. She, however, had several other friends that she enjoyed and often sat and danced with them as well.

Lillian was the one to make the inquiry about the nightlife.

Aleta suggested that they join her on Friday night at the bar that she often frequented. She said that she had several friends that she would introduce them to, and they could enjoy dancing and having a few drinks.

Lillian asked Laura if that sounded like something she would be interested in. Laura smiled and said that it would be a start, but she wanted to see more than just the nightlife and having a few drinks and some dancing at a bar.

Aleta said there was a Sunday concert at a local park happening on Sunday and she would show them the theater where throughout the year traveling troupes performed well known plays.

Laura said that would be a great help.

Before she left, Vajen had heard about the Sunday Concert in the park and figured that was an ideal time for an assault on the two daughters. She figured that was better than an attack on Lisa and her husband. She would make sure to instruct Wojciech to give the two a thorough beating. She already disliked them as much as their mother.

Once Vajen left, Lisa made a call to the department of Historical and Cultural Safeguarding. She introduce herself and asked to speak to the person in charge.

The support said that she would transfer her to Pieter Hoekstra, the current director.

The person that she was transferred to introduced himself and said that he had just reviewed her proposal and thought it was a good one and a clearer and simpler one than the one he had put on hold as he tried to decide whether to approve it. He asked what was going on to make Star Castle suddenly of interest.

Lisa said that she was not aware of any other proposal and then asked if it would help for them to meet in person to discuss her proposal. She said that his approval would be key in her decision to purchase the castle and make improvements.

She felt that she needed to better understand any requirements that applied to what she had in mind for the castle. She wanted to move quickly so that if it seemed feasible, she could quickly close on the purchase.

Pieter said that he only had time the following day and it had go be at his office.

Lisa agreed to meet him.

He transferred her back to his support person who let her know that she would have up to two hours on the following day. She then gave the address in The Hague and asked if there was anything else that Lisa needed.

Lisa wanted to laugh and say that she needed wings but kept quiet. After she hung up, she told Craig that they would need to leave right after lunch. She said that she was now happy that she had splurged and hired a full-time driver. She gave the driver the address of the hotel where she had originally planned to stay before they had agreed to cancel the visit to The Hague. She called ahead and confirmed two rooms.

Laura and Lillian wished her a good trip and said they had made plans with Aleta for the next couple of days and would remain at their current bed and breakfast.

Lisa smiled and told them that was great and wished them a good time.

Aleta had invited them to go out for drinks and she said they could walk through the entertainment area where there was a theater and several pubs that she often frequented. She laughed and said that it would give them an idea of the exciting nightlife of the area.

Both Laura and Lillian accepted and said that they appreciated the offer and looked forward to the evening out.

Lisa and Craig got ready to leave the castle and suggested they all go back to the hotel. They would then leave for The Hague.

Laura suggested to Aleta that they all go to lunch and afterwards they could all get ready for a night out. She made the point that the lunch and night out would be on her and Lillian.

Aleta said that arrangement fit her extremely low income well and then gave them the name and address of one of her favorite small restaurants where they could have lunch. She said that afterwards she would appreciate a ride back to their hotel.

Once back at the hotel, Lisa packed for a day trip and took off.

Laura, Lillian, and Aleta walked to the restaurant and discussed what they would do for the weekend.

Afterwards Lillian suggested the return to the hotel where she planned to work out in the small gym, and then take a nap.

Aleta said that she was going to go to where her current good friend Jacob worked to get him to invite his friends to the bar and grill that she had in mind for dinner and then some dancing.

Laura ended up laying on her bed reading a book with the title, "Murder on the Waterfront."

Aleta talked to Jacob and let him know that she was bringing two beautiful women with her to the bar and invited him to get the other two Js to join them that evening.

That evening as they walked through the downtown area with Aleta, both Laura and Lillian fired a continuous set of questions about the social life that was available in the surrounding area.

Aleta pointed out that there were several small villages that were within twenty kilometers of the castle. Each offered a different sort of shopping and nightlife. She volunteered to take them around to all of them. She said that she thought she could get Jacob to drive but suggested they buy the gas since it was the expensive part of them getting around.

She added that if the distance was increased to fifty or sixty kilometers the variety of fun things to do went up astronomically.

The more famous cities were all a few hours by train.

Lillian commented that it seemed that the location was actually one where you could go from quiet to loud depending on your mood.

Aleta agreed. She said that she was more for the quiet, but Europe was small enough that getting around was relatively easy.

She pointed to the sign over the night spot she was taking them to and said that it was the place that would have a small live group playing and it was a place that offered both dining in and then dancing.

As they were being led to their table, Laura commented that the place seemed to just be getting rolling for the evening.

Aleta nodded and said that the night life started in earnest after nine.

The waiter led them to a table for six.

Lillian looked at Aleta and asked who would be joining them.

Aleta grinned and said that she had invited three of her friends to a Dutch treat with three beautiful women.

Laura laughed and asked if they were to be the treat, or was she was talking about who paid for dinner.

Aleta shook her head and replied that she was talking about dinner.

When the three friends walked in, Lillian commented that perhaps she was willing to be the treat.

Aleta introduced the three as her 3Js, Jan, Jacob, and Johan.

Lillian sat down and was immediately drawn to Jacob.

Laura seemed to get along well with Jan.

Aleta was joking with all three of them, but it was Johan who she was most attracted to. So, she was pleased that the choices had been made in the manner that they had been.

Lillian was more interested in talking with Jacob and felt a connection that she had not anticipated. Jacob seemed interested in her life in the states and kept an easy conversation going.

It was clear to her that Laura was enjoying her conversation, but Lillian was not sure she was having the same feelings as she was. Her personal feelings were heightened by the person she was talking to.

As they finished the dessert Aleta pointed out that their timing seemed to be perfect because the band was starting to play, and the dance floor was clear.

Lillian accepted Jacob's invitation to dance. They were the first on the dance floor and she was impressed by Jacob's ability to lead her across the floor and then break off, dance separately and then take her back in his arms and move them smoothly along. It became clear as they danced that he was an accomplished dancer in both the modern and classical styles.

She looked around and realized that their group were the only couples on the dance floor. As the music ended the rest of the guests clapped.

It seemed that all 3J's were accomplished dancers.

As they returned to their table, Aleta commented that the clapping was for Lillian and Jacob and their excellent dancing.

<u>Chapter 7: Hook, Line and Sinker</u>

The evening ended on a high note. They all walked back to the hotel where Jan and Jacob said good night. They had agreed to attend the concert in the park together, but Jan said he had other plans.

Johan offered to drive Aleta home.

Laura and Lillian walked into the lobby and over to the elevator. Larua commented that Lillian and Jacob seemed to have hit it off.

Lillian smiled and said that being part of the Star Castle improvement team had just become a much more attractive proposition.

Laura agreed that the three were fun to be with and that she had fun, but she had obviously not made the same connection with Jan. She said that she enjoyed the evening more than the many that she had in New York. It was much more laid back and friendly. The environment was not as hectic.

Lillian agreed and added that Aleta had delivered on her promise to show them a good time. She was looking forward to the symphony in the park.

Aleta returned to the castle to find the "ghost" walking through the castle. She decided to take pictures and to take a picture of the boat that was tied up at the point used to enter the castle. She waited until the "ghost" returned to the boat and took several pictures. She figured that she would share the ghost story and who she thought was acting as the ghost with Laura and Lillian.

Lisa and Craig made it to The Hague and to the hotel where Lisa had originally made vacation reservations. She had been able to secure two rooms for the night. Her driver thanked her for her consideration.

During dinner Lisa let Craig know that she was ready to buy the Castle. If she got the support of the Director of Historical and Cultural Safeguarding, she would return and negotiate a deal with Vajen.

Craig let her know that he was all in, but he was not yet sure about the daughters.

Lisa said she hoped they would decide to be part of the transformation of the castle.

The next morning, they went to the office of Historical and Cultural Safeguarding to meet with Director Pieter Hoekstra.

The support secretary greeted them and said that Director Hoekstra was expecting them and led them into his office.

Lisa took in the rather tall grey-haired person in a black suit that was a contrast to his pink shirt and light lavender tie. She shook hands with him and introduced Craig. She thanked him for being kind enough to meet with her at such a short notice.

He nodded and said he had read her proposal, was interested in listening to her go through it and after her presentation he would share some more information about the situation he found himself in.

Lisa laid out her proposal package that had a series of annotated diagrams. As she shared the proposal, she made the point that she planned to progress slowly and make sure that the castle got refurbished section by section from the bottom up. She wanted to work with a local architect to maintain the castle's cultural integrity. She pointed out that it would take several years to accomplish what she had in mind. She commented that she had the resources to accomplish her plans and hoped to have the castle generate a positive cash flow in three years. She wanted the atmosphere of the castle to remain what she had experienced so far.

After Lisa finished her presentation Pieter said he was impressed with her proposal and asked if once she was done with the first phase, could he come and stay in one of the worker cottages.

Lisa smiled and said that his first stay would be on her. She knew at that point that she was going to get approved.

Pieter then shared that he had been hesitating on another proposal that was more general and had been put in by the realtor that claimed to be acting on behalf of the current owner, a distant cousin of the castle owner that had recently died. He had contacted that relative and found out that that relative was just expecting the agent to sell the property for more than a million and a half Euro and that he had no desire to renovate or do anything with the property. He was ready to move on with his life in New York City.

Lisa asked if he was willing to give her that person's name and phone number. She shared that she was apprehensive about the how the realtor was representing the property.

Pieter wrote the name and number on a sticky note and added the address of the person. He smiled and added that this relative was now located in New York, and she on the other hand was looking to move to The Netherlands from New York. He said it seemed that it was meant to be. He wished her good luck on making the purchase.

Lisa thanked him and said that she would contact him before going any farther with the realtor. She asked if there were any laws or regulations that the realtor might be breaking.

Pieter replied that the realtor would only break the law if she cheated the seller out of money. Since no money had changed hands, he was not aware of any law that had so far been broken.

Once they had left the office and were on their way back to the Castle, Craig volunteered to get one of his staff researching the situation to see if there was more going on at the castle then was obvious on the surface.

Lisa said that she would appreciate that and that she too felt that Vajen had a crooked iron in the fire and was up to more than was obvious. It was clear to her that Vajen did not want to sell the castle and most likely had some plan of her own that she was trying to implement.

She wondered out loud if there was some way to find out what that plan was and where Vajen was planning to get the financial support to make it happen.

When they got back to their hotel, they discovered that their two daughters were out for the evening with Aleta.

Lisa looked at Craig and said she hoped they would have a good time and meet some nice young men and get hooked on The Netherlands.

Craig said that would be great.

He then said he was going to make a call to his office to see how things were going and to ask one of his staff to find out how one might get funding for the improvement of a historical structure. He commented that knowing about such a source might help them manage their cash flow.

He was on the phone for a rather long time and when he hung up, he said they would have the information the following morning.

The next morning at breakfast the waiter guided them to a table and let them know that he had just served their daughters who had eaten and left with another person.

Lisa smiled and thanked him for the information and after going and getting her breakfast she sat down and commented that she had a good feeling about what was going on. She said that Aleta was proving to be an asset in the sense that she was showing the two daughters the nightlife and she was sure that today was going to be a day of shopping and some sightseeing.

Craig agreed and hoped they would find the area interesting and worth moving to.

Lisa nodded and said that would eliminate the concern she had about upsetting the great family relationship they all shared.

Aleta had chosen the day's shopping activities in such a way that they would make their way up one side of the river then cross and make their way back down the other side. She had gotten Johan to drive.

Lillian asked him about his friend Jacob and how long they had known each other.

Johan said that they had grown up in the same neighborhood along with Jan. They had been known as the three Js for as long as he could remember. All three families had lived in the same neighborhood for his entire life. They had vacationed all over Europe together.

Each family had a camper, and they would caravan to their destination and then camp. He commented that he and the other two Js had enjoyed every school break doing something interesting along the river or in one of the nearby parks.

Lillian asked if the other two Js had any close girlfriends.

Johan chuckled and said that Jacob was totally free of girlfriends, but Jan was currently seriously pursuing a young lady.

Laura nodded and thought about his cool behavior when she had made a pass at him. She smiled as she figured at least it was not her bad breath that had caused the cool behavior.

Throughout the day, Johan would drop the three off and then go to the end of the agreed shopping area. Later, after a full morning of shopping or at least letting the three walk the shopping area, he was more than ready to stop and have lunch.

Laura said that she and Lillian were paying for lunch and dinner, and everyone should go for whatever they wanted.

Aleta said she had both a lunch location and a dinner location in mind. The lunch location featured a wide variety of Asian cuisine. The dinner restaurant featured traditional Dutch cuisine.

Lillian asked Johan to invite the other two Js to dinner and that it was an American treat where the women paid.

Johan made the call. Jan declined because he had a date. Jacob agreed and asked what restaurant and what time.

Aleta spoke up and let him know the time and place.

Lillian was ready to call it a day for shopping and suggested that they just drive by the remaining shops. Laura agreed.

Aleta asked if they were up for a walk along the river and have lunch in one of the several lunch spots and enjoy the view of the boats going by.

Johan spoke up that lunch would be great no matter which spot they agreed to. He added that he needed a good walk after sitting in the car for most of the day.

Lunch was a hit, and the remaining time was spent driving by the remaining shops and then taking a ride into the countryside and stopping in one store where Aleta bought some cheese and pointed out all the cheeses that the store featured.

Laura said that she planned to buy several of the cheeses and said it was her treat and suggested that Johan pick his favorite cheese.

They then drove back to the restaurant they were going to for dinner.

They went in and ordered drinks. A few moments later Jacob arrived and came over to the table.

During dinner Laura noted that Lillian and Jacob had definitely hit it off. They chatted, joked, and laughed throughout the entire dinner.

Afterwards, Lillian let Laura know that she and Jacob were heading to one of his favorite night spots.

Laura said she hoped they had a great time, but she was going to return to the hotel.

The entire family met the next morning at breakfast. Lisa asked how the two were liking the area around the castle.

Lillian smiled and said that she was in hook, line, and sinker.

Laura shook her head and commented that what Lillian was into was a rather attractive guy named Jacob that she had met.

She then added that she was in because she found the social atmosphere much more enjoyable than the one in New York. She commented that it was more laid back and easy going.

Lisa then asked if the two could include a young boatman who she had invited and would be arriving that morning. Laura said that if he was willing to go to a concert in the park, she would be glad to include him.

Chapter 8: The Boatman

Dirk looked down along the canal as he sat in the boat's pilot seat. There were a variety of boats tied to each side. Some like his were designed to provide tours along the Amsterdam canals. Many were waterside homes. Some were lived in year around, but many were vacation homes. Like himself, the people of the canal had their own culture that was unique in that they preferred life on the water to life in a house and yard somewhere in the city. As he grew up, he had enjoyed both.

He, his brother, and their parents had a small home on the edge of what was now the historic downtown. His father had been a touring boatman on the canal as his father before him had been.

When school was in session, he would spend every weekend being the helper on his father's boat. During the breaks between school, he worked full-time. His father paid him, but he was required to save the majority of his pay for his continuing education. He knew the canals and all the stories about the history of the city by heart.

He had the grades that put him in the upper tier group of the university system. He attended the university and earned a degree in Business Administration.

When he graduated, he returned to the canals. He had saved enough money and was able to buy a boat from his father's friend who was retiring. It was a boat that rivaled the beauty of the boat his father had. His father's boat was made out a dark hard wood and the boat he bought was almost what he considered a blond color with streaks of dark brown running along the grain. During the next three years he struggled to keep his boat making money. He had refinished the boat and now when the sun hit it the reflection would make him squint. He knew he had one of the best-looking boats on the canal system and its beauty rivaled his fathers.

His father let him know that he had given a tour where he had given his business card to an American lady who was interested in getting a water tour along some river south of Amsterdam.

He was surprised that the next day he had received a call. He accepted the invitation to explore the possibility of providing boat tours along the Meuse River. He had no idea where the river was located and had to look it up. He figured it was worth looking into since he was currently struggling to keep his business in the black. He had spent his life savings on acquiring his boat and had borrowed heavily to advertise.

He felt that he needed a break and the offer to have exclusive rights for three years and to have his first year fully funded as if he had a full load of tourists throughout each week had convinced him to check out the situation. He was surprised to find out that his explorative visit would be totally paid for. This gave him a very positive feeling about the person he had talked to and the potential opportunity.

He left Amsterdam by train then later boarded a bus and finally took a taxi from the bus stop to the hotel address she had given him.

He was checking into the hotel when a rather good-looking lady introduced herself and asked if he was Dirk Van der Veen.

After the initial greeting, he was invited to have breakfast with her family.

He looked ahead as they walked back into the restaurant. He hoped they were going to sit down at the table where younger versions of the person who had introduced herself as Lisa were sitting.

He introduced himself and took the last open seat at the table that was across the woman that seemed to be the oldest of the two younger beauties.

Lisa introduced everyone and then suggested that he get his breakfast and they could then talk about his visit.

Dirk was thinking about how best to introduce himself and his business. He decided that he would introduce his boat, Griet, and talk about what he hoped to accomplish with his venture of giving water tours. This would allow him to both talk about himself and also to share his vision of growing his business.

Laura listened as Dirk described his struggles with getting his water tour business off the ground. She liked the enthusiasm that he had for the venture and his practical outlook at what he was trying to accomplish. She felt a connection with the low-key way he was describing the vision that was driving him.

Lillian smiled as she listened to Laura extract the details from Dirk about himself and about his business. It seemed to her that Laura was attracted to this Amsterdam boatman.

During breakfast Laura invited Dirk to the concert in the park. She was pleased when he accepted. She then extended the invitation to include a tour of Star Castle and afterwards if he had the time, she would ask her new friend Aleta to suggest a waterfront tour so he could see where he might give water tours of the area.

Dirk had been hesitant to make the trip but had been induced by the three-year exclusive contract offer and now he was hitting it off with an American beauty. He figured that the trip had already exceeded his expectations and the day had just started. He was happily looking at spending the rest of day with the beauty sitting across from him.

Lisa had listened to Laura and knew that by the end of the day she would have all of Dirk's life history. She hoped that Dirk would be smitten and agree to set up his business along the river. She would ask Aleta to suggest a place where Dirk could keep his boat.

She was hoping to coordinate his tour business with the startup of the castle's bed and breakfast.

Vajen got wind of the fact that Lisa had contacted the owner of the castle and had agreed to a sales price well below what she had set. She was so furious that she cursed for the rest of the day. She was now determined to make the life of the Roberts family as miserable and full of pain as possible.

She was happy that she had made the arrangements with the thugs from The Hague to beat up the persons she would target for them. She now changed her focus to the two daughters and would get them beat up. She figured that it would be more effective than having Lisa beat up. She called the leader of the thugs and told him about the change and that she wanted to have the women beat up and even cut up so that they would bleed and perhaps be disfigured. She wanted to have Lisa cry and to feel the pain that she was experiencing herself about the potential loss of ownership of the castle. She felt a thrill at being able to set up such an event.

She then invited Lisa over to her office to finalize the sale of the Castle with the intent of poisoning her and her husband. She would do all that was necessary to take control and be able to do whatever she wanted with the castle.

She had sympathized with Aleta's situation but had noticed that Aleta was now on very friendly terms with the two daughters. She planned to fire her as soon as she could.

After having set everything up she went out to enjoy the best dinner she could think of. She was envisioning all the things she had put into motion. She smiled as she sat and slowly sipped her favorite wine.

Aleta called to let Laura and Lillian know that she and Johan would be by to pick them up.

Laura asked if it would be any problem to add another person. She said that she had invited the person that was planning to set up boat tours along the river to join them.

Aleta said that would be no problem. She said she was looking forward to finding out what he had in mind for tours along the river.

Dirk excused himself and said that he would be back after getting his stuff to his room and changing into something more suitable for a day in the park. He asked if shorts and a sport shirt would be appropriate.

Luara stood up and pointed to her shorts and sandals and said he should join her.

Dirk nodded and said he got it. On the way to his room, he kept thinking that perhaps changing the venue to the small river and setting up business with a business arrangement with the Star Castle family was going to let him finally make the leap to a profitable business venture. He hope so because he was down to almost zero in his bank account.

After going to his room and changing, he returned to find Laura and Lillian waiting for him at the front desk.

They greeted him and then walked out to a waiting car where he was introduced to Aleta and Johan.

Aleta let them know that the concert would feature a local group known as The Golden Cellos that would open the concert. Then a full orchestra would feature "Mein Junges Leben Hat Ein End," "My young life has an end," by Jan Pieterszoon Sweelinck.

Dirk said that he was familiar with Sweelinck and that he liked his Pavana Lachrimae, the dance of my tears even more. He said that he figured it would be a very enjoyable outing.

Laura liked the fact that Dirk was a boatman that seemed to be well educated.

The car following them went unnoticed by the five.

After the girls left with Dirk, Lisa said that she was going to set up a meeting with Vajen after they got the information that Craig had asked his staff to dig up.

Craig said that he expected a call before noon. He hoped that his team would find some dirt on Vajen. He was convinced that she had worked herself up to the point where she was now hoping to take control of the castle. He wondered about what his team might find in her past.

Lisa nodded and said that Vajen was beginning to look like she was a scammer and it seemed to her that she was not representing the seller. She was not sure what the motive was, but it seemed that she was trying to discourage the sale.

Craig said that it seemed she was very experienced, and he bet his team would find something in the background check.

Once they arrived at the park, Aleta led the way to where the concert stage and the guest seating was set up.

They met up with Jacob and then took seats in the front row.

Lillian offered to buy snacks and drinks before the concert started.

Jacob said he would go and get whatever anyone wanted. Both Jan and Dirk said they would go along to help bring everything back. They agreed to a variety of snacks and large drinks. Lillian went along to pay.

After the four left, Aleta asked what Laura thought about Dirk and was he the type of person that would be an asset to the Star Castle project.

Laura smiled and said that it was too early to know whether he would be an asset. She added that she hoped so because so far, he was making a good impression on her.

Aleta smiled and commented that she hoped it would be a lucky day for another Dutch boy.

Laura replied that she hoped it would be a lucky day for another American woman.

Vajen had parked in the parking area two rows away and then followed the six of them to the concert area. She called her Polish thug, Wojciech and informed him where he and his gang would find the two that she wanted to have roughed up.

She waited patiently for him and his gang to arrive. She pointed out the location of the parked car that their targets were driving and then walked them to the area in the park where the concert was now being performed. She pointed out the two women that she wanted roughed up and if they were cut up or had broken bones, she would add a bonus.

Wojciech made sure he had the right two. He then took in the fact that there were only a few police present and they seemed to be focused on providing security for the people on the stage. He then walked slowly back to the parking lot. He had his car moved as close to the exit as possible. He wanted to be gone before the police could respond.

He hoped that his targets would be among the last to be leaving. He found a spot, hidden by a row of bushes where he and the five members of his gang could sit and wait. He sent one of gang to keep an eye on their targets.

Vajen wished she could stay and take pictures but decided she would enjoy the beat-up condition of the two on the following day. She was sure that getting beat up and perhaps disfigured would convince the family to give up their idea of buying the castle. Just the thought of it sent her emotions to a peak.

When the concert ended Aleta suggested they wait while most people left. She asked if they would like to go from the park for a walk along the river front. She added that there was a rather enjoyable sandwich shop that had tables overlooking the river that might give Dirk an idea about his boat business.

They all agreed that the walk to the sandwich shop sounded appealing and followed Aleta and Johan and walked toward the river.

Wojciech watched as the parking lot emptied and there were only a few cars left. He wondered where his scout happened to be.

He was just about to send someone else out to see what was going on when his scout came jogging in.

When he was told where the two targets had gone, he led the way to his car and had his driver find the way to the restaurant and park the car for an easy getaway.

He decided to take a seat a few tables away from his targets and then ordered a beer for everyone.

Lillian's seat gave her a direct view of the six guys that had come out to the patio. It seemed to her that they were watching her table. She didn't say anything but the hair on the back of her neck stood up. It seemed too obvious to her. She figured them for some sort of gang or at least troublemakers.

The conversation at her table focused on the river traffic and speculation on whether a river tour business was viable.

She relaxed but kept her eyes on the six rough looking guys watching them.

Aleta said there were several restaurants along the river that would most likely love to offer those taking a river tour specials on lunch or dinner. She said that she would be glad to point them out.

Johan added that there were numerous smaller attractions along the river that might be of interest.

Jacob commented that he and the other 2J's had often played on the ruins of an ancient bridge that he thought would be of interest.

Dirk suggested that he give them all a ride on the Meuse after he brought the Griet down from Amsterdam and they could suggest the route that he should use for his guided tour. He said that he would capture their dialogue on that boat ride so he could develop the tour script.

The day was near sunset when they all decided to return to their car.

Lillian noticed that the six guys sitting a few tables away asked for their bill at the same time that Laura asked for theirs. She was now sure they had been watching for the last couple of hours.

She smiled as she gave Laura their special encouragement word "Kōun o" which meant "good luck." This was their personal word that they always shared before a Tae Kwon Do match.

Laura looked at her curiously but nodded her head. "Yes, win or lose," she replied with a smile. She was now on full alert.

They had just gotten up to walk back to the car when the attack happened. Two of the attackers knocked Aleta, Johan, Jacob, and Dirk down. The biggest thug pointed and told them to stay down. The other pointed a gun at them and told them that they should stay down and not get hurt.

The other four attacked Laura and Lillian.

Laura saw the attacker's knife in one hand and the club in the other. She guided the knife's hand past her face and then pushed hard and guided it into the arm holding the club. The knife went in all the way to the hilt. She grabbed the club as it dropped and then went then went down flat to the ground and delivered a round house kick to the second attacker's rib cage. She knew that she had delivered the kick as hard as she had intended when she heard the ribs crack. She jumped up and hit the second attacker on the side of the head with the club. He went down on his butt.

The first attacker was getting ready to shoot her, but she hit him in the throat, and he dropped his gun. He staggered back, choking, then he turned and ran toward the parking lot.

She looked over to where Lillian had done something similar and was getting ready to stand up.

The attacker with the cracked ribs called out to the person holding the gun to shoot the bitches.

As that person turned to shoot, Dirk did a snap jump to his feet and pushed the arm holding the gun down and away and pulled the gun from his hand. He heard a snap and figured he had broken the trigger finger.

The thug who had knocked the four down shouted they should hightail it. Picked up one of the thugs who had been knocked out by Lillian and all six ran away as fast as they could.

Dirk looked around and decided not to chase after them. He walked over to Laura and asked if she was alright.

Laura gave him a hug and thanked him for attacking the shooter. She then gave him a kiss.

Dirk smiled, nodded, and wondered who had set them up.

The restaurant owner came over and said that he had never had something like that happen at his restaurant. He let them know that he had called the police.

He then offered to provide some snacks and drinks while they waited for the police to arrive.

Aleta said that she and Johan were going to go and bring the car to the restaurant.

Lillian called her father and explained what had occurred and told him to be on the lookout for some sort of attack.

She was happy to hear him say that he would let the hotel security know.

Craig had heard from his team that had looked into Vajen's background. They reported that she had a history of petty crimes and had been in jail repeatedly in her younger years for shoplifting and stealing. She seemed to have found legitimate work as a realtor with only a few complaints. They had also found out that her recent relationship with the deceased Star Castle owner had caused the local pathologist to initially be suspicious of foul play. But nothing was found to confirm his suspicion, so no charges were filed.

Lisa had been listening and after Craig hung up, she suggested that they arrange a meeting with Vajen, at her office. She wanted to see if she could trick Vajen into giving herself away. She wondered if Vajen had graduated to the crime of murder.

She shared an idea she had that might trigger Vajen to give herself away.

<u>Chapter 9: Denial</u>

Vajen listened quietly as Wojciech angrily described what had happened. He was almost shouting as he told her he wanted twice what she had promised him for the attack. He said he was leaving the area but planned to stop by and collect the additional money before leaving. Vajen had the money, but she had planned to keep the bonus she had offered for herself. She figured it would be better to give it to him to keep him quiet and get him out of the area. She was also afraid to have him, and his gang attack her. She could not believe that two women had overcome the gang she had hired.

She asked him how badly the two women had been hurt.

He asked her if she had listened to what he had just told her. His guys were the ones that were hurt. One was having trouble talking from having had his larynx smashed. One had eyes that were bloody red from having fingers poked into them. One was hobbling on his left leg. His gunman had a broken finger. He was sure he had a cracked rib and the lump on the side of his head ached like mad.

His biggest guy was the only one that had walked away unscathed. He finished by saying that the two women were the deliverers of all the hurt.

Vajen told him to come by and she would give him the money.

He told her he would honk, and she could hand him the money through the window of his car, and he would drive on.

When she heard the honk, Vajen took the money bag out to the car. As she leaned down to look in through the passenger side window, a flash went off. She realized that her picture had been taken by the person behind the driver's wheel.

Wojciech smiled at her and let her know that her picture was insurance in case she tried to say she had never seen him.

Vajen stood, for a minute, as she watched the car drive away. Things had not worked out the way she had anticipated. She had never suspected that the two young women knew some sort of martial arts. She decided that she would forget about the two daughters and focus on Lisa and her husband.

She received a call from Lisa and agreed to a meeting at her office to conclude the sale of Star Castle. She figured that it would give her the opportunity to use the left-over poison she had used on the old lady who had owned the castle. She was sure that she had enough that would suffice to eliminate them many times over.

Once the meeting was over, she would immediately leave for the coast and would be far enough away that she could deny any connection with their death. She was now looking forward to finalizing the sale. She would use fake papers so that she would leave the sale open and then she would file the paperwork for her ownership.

Aleta and the rest of the group had been at the restaurant for over an hour as two local police officers interviewed them.

It turned out that the restaurant owner had the best overall description of what had happened. He said that it was like a scene out of a movie where the bad guys were overwhelmed by two women moving at lightning speed in a devasting assault dance on their attackers. He figured the attackers were all limping away with a variety of wounds in less than two minutes. One had a knife in his arm, and another had to be led away because he could not see. The two that had pulled guns limped to the parking lot. One was holding his right hand as he ran and the other was coughing as he ran toward the parking lot. The biggest thug carried someone over his shoulder, as he trotted to the parking lot. When asked if he had gotten the make of car or license plate number the owner said that he had not seen the car.

Dirk and Laura took the officer interviewing them to where the guns lay on the ground.

Lillian went along and pointed to a straight razor and a butterfly knife that her two assailants had dropped.

Laura and Lillian then described their actions when the attack took place. The officer asked where they had learned their martial arts. Laura answered that the two of them and their father had all gone together to Tae Kwon Do classes at the YMCA since they had become teenagers.

He commented that it had paid off.

The two officers said that they were pleased that no one in the group was hurt and said that they would come by to the hotel with the official report the next day.

They then tapped off the area and asked the owner to make sure no one went into the taped off area until the forensics team took down the tape.

A few minutes later, Aleta and Johan came over to Laura with several bags in hand and said that the restaurant owner had given each of them his best carry out dinner and had invited them back.

Dirk shared that he had briefly described bringing lunch and dinner guests via boat and said that the owner was very interested in such a business venture. He planned on returning the next day to see what kind of business arrangements they could make.

Laura smiled and complemented Dirk for making lemonade.

The comment puzzled him until Lillian explained what it meant.

He laughed and said that he was more familiar with, "Every cloud has a silver lining," or "After the rain, comes the good weather," or "An evil sometimes turns out to be a blessing in disguise."

Laura nodded and said she liked all of the sayings. She took his arm and the two of them walked to the car.

They all got in the car and drove to the hotel. The three got out when they got to the hotel.

Aleta let them know that she was going back to the castle.

Lisa had left a note at the desk that she and Craig were in the dining area relaxing and discussing the next steps on the project.

Dirk excused himself and said he would eat his carry out in his room, he wanted to prepare for his meeting with the restaurant owner.

Lillian and Laura went into the dining area and joined their parents.

Lisa asked about the incident at the restaurant.

Laura said that she had been surprised by Lillian's encouragement that they always gave each other before a Tai Kwon Do match but when the thugs attacked both of them went, into action and easily inflicted hurt and pain on the attackers who then fled.

She added that she was impressed by Dirk's bravery in attacking one thug who had a gun. She commented that the bullet meant for one of the two of them went into the ground as Dirk pushed the gun down. The gunman ran away holding his gun hand. She figured Dirk had broken his finger when he pulled that gun from his hand.

Craig said he was proud of all of them. He commented that there seemed to be only one reasonable explanation for the attack and that was to discourage them from buying the castle. He made the point that there seemed to be only one person that would benefit and go to the length of having them attacked.

Lisa said that she had set up a meeting the following day with Vajen and was working with the local police to see if she could get a confession out of her about the attack and her desire to discourage them from buying the castle.

Vajen spent the evening and part of the night going through several potential scenarios to eliminate Lisa and her husband. She had accepted meeting them in her office to discuss the closing on the purchase of the Castle. She decided that she would use the remainder of the poison she had used on the old lady that had owned the castle. She would put the poison in the wine she planned to offer in celebration of closing the sale. She figured she would be on the coast by the time the poison finally killed them.

The next morning Lisa was at the police station where she was outfitted with a listening device. The attack the previous day had convinced the local police to work with her. They still remembered the coroner's suspicion of foul play associated with the death of the previous owner. They counseled Lisa to face Vajen when talking to her so they could get the best reception from the microphone she would be wearing.

They let her know if the meeting became violent, they would rush into the room.

She and Craig then went to Vajen's office. It was their first time to be invited to it. Both she and Craig were impressed with its opulence. The room looked more like a book lined lawyers office with all the classical books turned front cover out. There was one shelf behind the desk with a large collection of the small Delft Blue houses. The Cherrywood desk had a series of small ceramic Greek statues arranged along the edge.

It was clear to the two of them that Vajen had her office arranged and decorated to impress the customer. She was clearly projecting success.

Vajen greet them and pointed to a table that was matched to the desk and suggested they sit down and process the paperwork to close the deal on the castle.

Lisa took the seat closest to Vajen. She noted the wine class in front of each of them. She asked what kind of red wine they were going to celebrate with.

Vajen replied that it was, Chateau Pontet-Canet Grand Cru Classe, Pauillac, one of the premier Dutch wines that she had brought out for the occasion. She would have liked to have added that it also masked the flavor of the poison the best.

She smiled and went methodically through the paperwork and pointed to the X's where a signature was required.

Lisa said that she was looking forward to enjoying the wine when they celebrated closing on the sale of the Castle.

Vajen smiled and said that she too was looking forwards to celebrating the sale.

Lisa returned the smiled and then suggested that they first talk about Vajen's failed attack on her daughters.

Vajen acted as if she was shocked. She did not have to do any acting because she had not expected to have the attack so quickly linked to her and she was alarmed and surprised at the question. She was glad that she already had the poison in the wine glasses.

She denied knowing anything about the thugs that had done such a thing.

Lisa shook her head and asked how she knew that some thugs were the attackers.

Vajen was silent for a moment, she shook her head and replied that she had assumed that it would be more than one attacker.

Craig asked her about the land sales scam she had tried a few years ago in the Apeldoorn region as he lifted his wine glass as if to take a sip.

Vajen hesitated to see if he would take a drink. Then she replied she did not know what he was talking about. She was now aware that the meeting was not going to go as she had envisioned. She thought about the three fifty seven revolver she had in the top drawer of her desk.

Craig then shared that he had discovered she had multiple arrests for shoplifting and some other minor crimes and wondered what scam she was trying to pull on them. He pushed the official looking reports toward her.

He pretended to take a small sip of wine and commented that its flavor was dark and incisive.

Vajen smiled as she replied that she had indeed had a problem during her younger years but that had ended when she realized that being a realtor would provide her with a good life. She commented that she had been in the realty business for over fifteen years and had an unblemished record.

Lisa switched glasses with Vajen and to took a small sip of the wine and commented that it had robust and fruity flavor.

She looked at Vajen and lifted her glass and as she pushed a check of €112,500 Euro across to Vajen. She suggested a toast to closing the sale.

Vajen knew she could not drink a toast with the wine in the glass that was now in front of her. She looked at the check and commented that she thought they were closing on the asking price of two and a half million Euro and that the check should be €187,500 not €112,500 Euro.

Lisa shook her head and said that actually they had already settled with the owner and had the closing papers in their possession and that all they needed now was to receive the title from the land office.

Vajen was furious. She jumped up and called Lisa a bitch. Lisa smiled and said that coming from her, it might be a compliment. She then asked how Vajen had gotten away with poisoning the old woman who owned the castle. Vajen replied that there was no way to prove such a thing.

Craig held up his glass and said that whatever she had put in his glass would prove that she had poisoned the owner so that she could gain possession of the castle.

Vajen rushed to her desk and pulled out her gun.

Craig jumped up on the table and launched himself through the air. He threw the wine glass at Vajen and noted that it hit between the eyes. He grabbed her hand and twisted it, so the gun pointed away to his left as Vajen repeatedly pulled the trigger.

The two officers rushed into the room as the repeated roar of the three fifty seven was occurring.

He hit the top of her desk and slid across and hit her in the head with his right elbow and then tried to slow down as he went headfirst into the cabinet and shelves behind the desk.

Books and the small Delft Blue houses rained down on him from above.

He heard Vajen right arm snap as he landed full force on it. He also noted that he had broken her hand when he had twisted the gun from her hand.

He was dazed, on the verge of passing out and was not aware that in sliding across the desk one of the statutes had cut a gash on his thigh and he was bleeding.

He had landed with the left leg rising up the drawer side of the desk and the other laying flat on the floor.

The officer has immediately put pressure on the wound and told him not to move.

Craig let him know that was sitting on Vajen's arm that he was sure was broken in multiple places.

The officer helped him move over and lie down on the floor.

Two EMT persons came into the room and began checking on both Craig and Vajen.

One of them commented that Vajen's right arm was broken in multiple places, and she also had broken bones in her right hand.

Vajen came awake as her arm was contained in an arm cast so that she could be taken to the local hospital.

She looked at Craig and said she hoped he would die in pain.

Craig smiled and said the poisoned red wine he had thrown at her had gone in her face, her eyes and her mouth and she was the one that most likely would be the one to die.

The lead EMT person asked what kind of poison they were talking about.

Craig said he had no clue, and they should ask Vajen.

They found the empty bottle of poison and then after getting her to the restroom administered a medicine to cause Vajen to throw up and they also flushed her eyes out with a saline solution and washed her face.

Vajen was screaming and cursing during the entire time. The EMT's finally gave her a sedative to quiet her down.

As Vajen was being put into the ambulance to be taken to the hospital, Lisa exposed her wire and let Vajen know she had confessed to the murder of the Star Castle owner and her attempt at killing the both of them.

Vajen let out a scream and tried to spit at Lisa. Then she shouted that she was firing Aleta and would not pay her for the last month. "Screw all of you, she shouted as she was lifted into the emergency van.

Lisa gave Craig a hug and said she would have to call him Dirk for being willing to go for the thug with the gun. She pointed to the huge holes in the floor, gave him another hug and said he was as brave as Dirk.

The EMT said that his team would take him to the local hospital where he would have his leg looked at.

The rest of the day was spent having the wound on his thigh treated. It took eight sixteen stitches to close the wound and he was told to take it easy.

He went back to the hotel and enjoyed a dinner in bed in his room.

Laura, Lillian, Aleta all came to his room and brought him a gift. Lillian gave him a new pair of trousers to replace the one that had been ruined.

That evening Craig let Lisa know that he would have his team send the information they had on Vajen when they learned who the prosecutor was. He said that with her background, her attempt to poison them, her basic confession to killing the previous owner and the drinks spiked with the poison, would make it easy for the prosecutor to get a conviction. He would have his lawyer participate to ensure that the court would go for the maximum penalty.

Lisa said they should get everyone together for a celebration dinner. She said they should get reservations at the restaurant where the kids had been attacked.

<u>Chapter 10: Aftermath</u>

Lisa worked with the owner of the restaurant to set up a special celebration. She asked to have the entire restaurant reserved for her party. She also worked with him on what the menu should be. He agreed to having all the ingredients be local. He said that one of his friends ran the butcher shop in town and would be able to provide everything and he would buy the fruits and vegetables from the local farmer's market.

She invited Aleta's parents and the three 3J's and Dirk's parents. She arranged for her and Craig's parents to come over. She made sure they had first class tickets. She figured this would be a once in a lifetime type of event and she wanted to let her parents know how decadent she had become.

Craig had arranged for his lawyer and wife to attend, and he had let the rest of his consulting group know that they would all get a trip over when Star Castle opened for business.

Lisa hired a small group to play music.

The event was a resounding success, and she was sure that what she had set out to do, which was to transition to a new family life that kept her family together, was now going to happen.

Laura went with Dirk to Amsterdam to get his boat and bring it back.

It had become clear to Lisa that the two had hit it off and had a wonderful relationship.

The same was true with Lillian and Jacob who seemed to do everything together.

Aleta approached her and asked if she would be keeping her job as groundskeeper.

Lisa asked her to go for a walk. As they walked along, she said that she was promoting Aleta to run a grounds keeping crew of four and that it was up to Aleta to supervise the dredging of the mote and to design and arrange to have flower beds around the grounds of the castle and to have additional walking paths put in.

She then offered a salary that she knew was at least three times Aleta's current salary retroactive to the day that they had first talked on the phone.

Aleta stopped and said she might have misheard the salary and that what she heard was more than she had ever been paid.

Lisa responded that she expected the excellent work that Aleta had been doing to continue and that as the groundskeeper crew leader she expected the best. She wanted the grounds around the castle to make the news in the coming year as one of the most beautiful places to visit.

She added that it was up to Aleta to hire and supervise the additional ground keepers and to work with a park designer to turn the grounds into one of the main attraction for Star Castle.

Aleta had tears in her eyes as she gave Lisa a hug. She said that she never felt so good about being around everyone in her family.

Lisa let her know that she was thought of as family.

Aleta asked if she could continue to live in the castle.

Lisa said that eventually they would all have suites in the castle itself and until then Aleta was welcome to continue to live where she was currently living.

Both Lillian and Laura had asked about using one of the work huts to live in.

Lisa hired a local contractor to come in and renovate three additional cottages. She had them look at Aleta's cottage and asked them to use it as a model but to also suggest improvements and that any improvements were to be added to Aleta's cottage. She made the point that these first cottages would be the model for the remaining cottages.

Dirk and Laura had returned with his boat, and he had insisted that the first river boat tour would be for the eight people that he considered the Star Castle family. He had arranged the best snacks that he and Laura could think of. They had selected shrimp, lobster tail cocktail, a variety of sliced meats, and a large tray of local fruits and vegetables. There was beer, wine, and a variety of soft drinks.

The tour began at a dock that also had a shed-like cover on one side to house the boat. Dirk guided the Griet upriver for about an hour on the castle side and then went down towards Star Castle on the other side. The view of the Castle was the highlight of the tour.

Lisa could easily see the flag that she had flying from the spot where she had stood at the top wall and had realized that she had found what she had been looking for.

The renovation of the twenty-four cottages took over six months. During that time Lisa and the family had worked with a series of companies to examine and determine the required structural work required to repair the base and the castle itself.

Aleta had the mote drained and the mud removed. The mud removal took longer than anticipated because human remains had been discovered and a group of anthropologists came in to carefully remove the bones. Each body had been weighted with chain or with boulders. The oldest body was some twelve hundred years old. The bones had been preserved by the mud that kept the oxygen away.

Once the mud was removed from between a star point, the repair work was done and then that section was once again filled with water. Aleta had arranged for each section to be separated from the ones still under repair so that the water could be reintroduced. She had learned that it was important to keep the water around the base of the star points to ensure the stability of the star base.

Lisa became the general supervisor but each of the family members had their specific focus areas.

Craig and Laura were working with a general contractor and a series of special design organizations to design the interior living areas. The eight towers each had seven floors and each floor required a great deal of work. The first focus was ensuring the integrity of the tower structure. Then the first tower to be renovated and converted to a bed and breakfast was selected.

The family had agreed on the goal of renovating one tower every other year. This meant that it would take at least sixteen years to renovate the entire castle.

Aleta finished getting the mud removed from the mote, the base of the star repaired and the first walking path around the perimeter of the property completed in the first year. She had made sure that the fish that had been in the mote had been rescued and when the mote was refilled, she released all of them back. She also made sure that the water lilies that had been in the mote were reintroduced. The final touch was to release the two pair of black swan and their goslings.

She held a celebration picnic that featured a small pig on a spit as the main course and all the special dishes that her parents had brought down.

Lisa congratulated her and announced that she was giving her a pay raise for the excellent work she had done.

It was during the picnic that Johan proposed to Aleta.

He was followed by Jacob proposing to Lillian.

Then Dirk proposed to Laura.

It was clear that the three had conspired to coordinate their proposals.

Lisa and Craig gave each other a hug as they listened to the acceptances.

They asked where the honeymoons were going to be and were surprised that the three had all decided to have a destination wedding in Hawaii and afterwards spend their honeymoon together there.

Lisa jokingly suggested that Star Castle could also host a destination wedding.

Laura replied that indeed it could, but she planned to return and live in it but felt that a first-class trip to Hawaii sound marvelous to her.

After the picnic, Lisa decided she would take a walk around the perimeter of the property. She and Craig were holding hands as they walked.

She took in the flower gardens, the clouds drifting overhead and the sun slowly sinking toward the horizon. She put her arm around Craigs back and let him know how happy she was that their daughters had found the same relationship that the two of them enjoyed.

Craig nodded and said that her idea about moving the family to a new environment that let them enjoy what they did and still have time to grow intellectually and emotionally had been an ultimate success.

<u>Chapter 11: Ten Years Later</u>

Star Castle's success as a bed and breakfast exceeded all expectations. The project was accelerated, and all eight towers were converted and maintained at a more than eighty percent fill rate. The décor of each tower represented a specific one one-hundred-year time period from the time of its original construction to the present. Every tower was as close to authentic as could be managed.

Fishing in the large tanks at the very top wall water tanks, in the mote from either the bridge or boats in the mote and at the river Meuse where the water feed for the mote originated was available for those desiring to fish. The novelty of such a variety of fishing locations was one of the features that seemed to attract many of the repeat customers.

Powering the bucket lift that brought the water up from the river allowed those interested in that experience as much time as they desired. A motor operated the bucket lift during the time no one was doing it and at night to keep the mote full but served as a tourist attraction during the day.

Aleta had succeeded beyond expectations and the Star Castle gardens won multiple awards for best originally themed garden. Local residents were allowed free entry. The Gardens became an attraction that Dirk used as a part of his water boat tour business. His customers were the only ones except local residents and castle guests that got to tour the gardens.

A luncheon was held every day and rotated from luncheon spots at the point of each Star and featured the foods associated with that tower's time period. The size of the luncheons was based on reservations that were put in by guests the day before.

Walking tours of the castle and the grounds left on a fifteen-minute schedule throughout the day starting at sunrise and going to sunset. The tours had guides that told the historic story of Star Castle from how the choice for its star shape had been made and how the builder had made his fortune by imposing one of the oldest known taxes on the merchant river boat traffic. The tours that went around the edge of the property stopped numerous times at refreshment stands that provided drinks and snacks that took those walking through the experience of the drinks and snacks that were available during each epoch of time. There were short, intermediate and the long tours that all operated in the same manner.

The twenty-four small exterior cottages enjoyed an almost one hundred percent occupancy. They were the only units where guests could choose to cook their own meals. The attraction was that the desired food could be ordered, and the order was delivered within an hour at no additional expense.

All guests had a choice of the common eating areas present on the first level of each tower. Each tower featured different menu choices based on the time period associated with that tower. Guest could make reservations to eat in any tower.

There was an evening movie showing three times during the week and each evening there was other live entertainment. Each guest room featured a large screen that provided additional evening entertainment.

Dirk's river boat tour fleet now sported five tour boats. Three boats were more or less duplicates of the Griet, his original boat, but he had two boats that carried forty guests at a time. Every restaurant along the river had a contract with him. The arrangements worked well because only a few restaurants could accommodate the larger boats and the rest of the restaurants were featured on specific days of the week.

He had purchased the land along the bank where he had built four docks. Three had sheds where he periodically pulled the three smaller tour boats out of the water and cleaned their hulls.

The fourth dock was where his two bigger tour boats docked when they were not out giving tours.

The boats were all cleaned after each tour and then received a detailed cleaning at the end of each day.

His younger brother managed the two large tour boats and lived in the house that was part of the riverside property and his brother's children attended a nearby school to which they were able to walk.

He, Laura and their two children lived in the family tower. The two children, a boy named Lieke now eight and girl named Emma Lisa now seven, both attended classes in a nearby school and caught the bus where the castle property met the small highway running by.

Laura had transitioned from being the general contractor managing all the internal construction to being in charge of maintaining all the infrastructure and doing any upgrades and repairs in the entire Star Castle complex. The last upgrade had been the eighth floor central tower where the family often met to enjoy the setting sun. This tower level was a family only location.

Laura's current project was the construction of an amphitheater in the back of the property. This area had been selected because it was a very empty part of the property but was an easy walk from the castle and the parking lot that was available for the local population once the amphitheater was completed. Then a Sunday concert would be featured during the warm season.

Lillian was the financial manager of the finance group that she managed. Her group met once a week in person but operated the rest of the time virtually. She had two group members that were far enough away that they only met in person once a quarter. One remote member lived in Amsterdam and was the interface with the bank the Star Castle account there and the other was located in Rotterdam and had a similar role interfacing with the Star Castle account at a bank there.

She and Jacob had three children, the oldest, Sanne, now nine was very much like her in both looks and in personality, Dael, now eight was the athletic one and enjoyed soccer, and Eva Lisa now seven and best friend to Emma. They both loved the fact that they had their grandmother's name for their middle names.

Jacob had become an accomplished piano player and had spent two years in Amsterdam where he played with the Royal Concertgebouw Orchestra, considered one of the leading worldwide orchestras. He chose to leave it to come back to become the featured pianist at Star Castle so he could be with the family and be in the country that he had grown up in and loved.

Vajen had received a life sentence and been sent to the maximum-security prison Pi Vught. She was not in the most secure part with the most dangerous prisoners, but she was very much aware of the tremendous loss of freedom.

She tried to scam some of the other prisoners but after having been beaten up she chose a lower profile. Her one enjoyment was reading but she was not sure she would be able to continue living the life she was now limited to.

She had limited weekly tv privileges and was furious when she caught one advertisement about the beauty and wonders of Star Castle. It seemed that every time she watched she caught another report about the splendid castle and the surrounding countryside. She knew that it was a countryside she would never again see. She remained bitter for the rest of her life.

Lisa stood at the seventh level at the same spot where she had first stood when she had decided that she had found what she was looking for. She still did not know that it was the exact spot where the first owner and builder of the castle had stood as he took in the flat fields that flowed to the horizon and the river with its boat traffic. She was enjoying that exact view and experiencing a similar feeling of accomplishment.

Her daughters all had a similar bond to the one she had with Craig. She was now a grandmother eight times and two of her grandchildren carried her name. She was pleased that two of the boys had Craig as a middle name as well.

Craig's business in the US had continued being very lucrative and the business owned a third of the Castle. He had followed through and made the castle a yearly paid vacation spot for his entire company.

He worked locally with several companies and had managed the structural repair work that after ten years was still under way.

The castle had crossed the profitability threshold in the three years she had targeted. She had crossed that threshold by a mere one thousand dollars, but she had crossed it.

Director Pieter Hoekstra, that at that time had recently retired, had not only been one of her first guests but he was present to tease her about the huge one thousand dollar profit she had finally achieved. Now as she stood taking in the setting sun, he sadly was in hospice care awaiting the setting of his sun.

Craig, his hair still full but now a silver grey gave her a hug and offered a penny for her thoughts.

She replied that he was a few million dollars short but if he gave her kiss, she would let it go by.
They kissed just as the sun set and turned the bottom of the clouds a shimmering red.

The End

__About the Author__

Ronald E. Mueller
remwriter95@gmail.com

Ron grew up in what is now Flint River State Park in Southeast Iowa. The 170-year-old house Ron lived in is built into a hillside. It faces a 125-foot-high cliff towering over the little Flint River. The house and the land talked to him about; the passing of time, the struggle to conquer the land, the struggles people faced and the wonder of nature.

He climbed the cliffs, crawled into the caves, dove from the swimming rock, collected clams from the bottom of the pond, gigged and skinned frogs for their legs. He trapped muskrats for fur, hunted raccoon in the dead of night, and with only a stick hunted rabbits in the dead of winter.

His young life was outdoors, and nature tested him.

He walked to a one room stone schoolhouse uphill both ways. A stern but warm-hearted teacher, Mrs. Henry was instrumental in shaping his character as she shepherded him from the fourth to the eighth grade. A Montessori before its time. It was a great way to grow up.

His experiences inter-twined with snippets of fantasy lend themselves to the adventures he leads the reader through.

Star Mote Castle

Ron Mueller

Published by: Around the World Publishing LLC.

QR Links to

ATWP.US web site